FIGHT OR FLY

The Secret Pack Trilogy

Hide or Die
Fight or Fly
Truth or Lie

The Packverse Trilogy

All for Knot: Book One
All for Knot: Book Two
Knot for Sale

The Knot Playing Fair Trilogy

Knot Playing Fair: Book One
Knot Playing Fair: Book Two
Knot Your Victim

FIGHT OR FLY

EMBER BLAZE

Fight or Fly (Secret Pack, #2)

ISBN: 978-1-955073-24-0 (paperback)

For information, contact the publisher at www.otherlovepublishing.com/contact/

First Edition: December 2021

Author's Note

Secret Pack is a human omegaverse trilogy where the main character doesn't have to pick one person in the end. It features protective alphas and the omegas who love them, but no shifters. The series is intended for a mature audience.

Table of Contents

ONE

Leona

IN RETROSPECT, doing vodka shots with an alpha might not have been the best decision I'd ever made. Though in my defense, there were times when vodka was, without a doubt, the right response to a situation. This was, I felt pretty sure, one of those times.

A copy of *The New York Times* lay on the table between us, the front page dominated by a candid photo of me taken at the bilateral summit a mere couple of weeks ago. I looked harried and exhausted. Probably because I'd been, well… *harried and exhausted.*

"It's not even a good picture," I said, listlessly dragging my refilled shot glass toward me.

HIGH-LEVEL MEMBER OF UFNA FOREIGN OFFICE ARRESTED, the headline screamed. *UNREGISTERED OMEGA ESCAPES POLICE CUSTODY.*

Alex gave me a narrow look as she refilled her own glass with a hand that seemed way steadier than it should be. "Would it improve the situation if they'd used a professional headshot instead?"

I lifted my arm in a sloppy wave. "I'm vain," I told her. "Kam's vain. We're both vain omegas, and if I'm gonna be plastered across every single front page in the country, I'd rather look good doing it, damn it."

On the positive side—if there was one—the article made absolutely no mention of Kam, my fellow omega-in-hiding. Rhys Beckett got about an inch of dedicated column space, since he'd signed his own name to the forged paperwork he'd used to get me out of Montreal police custody. Alex's boss hadn't exactly been subtle when he'd strode in, utterly shameless, and wielded his status as a federal security agent like a bludgeon.

Ex-federal security agent, now. He was a fugitive like the rest of us, though he appeared largely unconcerned by that fact. I got the impression Beckett had cycled through a few different identities over the course of his lifetime. Like me... like Kam... he was an omega hiding in a beta-dominated world. But first and foremost, he was involved in the underground—the shadowy association of alphas, omegas, and beta allies that helped hide and protect our people from persecution in a world ruled by beta supremacists.

He'd helped Kam and me, even if I still wasn't totally sure why. He said he wanted us to join the underground. He said we could still make a difference there. And his alphas... *they* wanted to court us. To join our packs together; maybe to mate. At least, Jax and Flynn did. I got the impression my current drinking companion would rather chop off her right hand than get emotionally tangled up with a pair of fugitive omegas.

She gestured at me with her shot glass and tipped it up, swallowing the contents with a sharp tilt of her head. "Bottoms up," she said, setting the now-empty glass firmly back on the table and reaching for the bottle. "You're not nearly drunk enough yet."

I peered at her through bleary eyes. "How do you know?"

"You haven't asked me the question you want to ask me," she replied.

And... *fair*.

I tipped the vodka down my throat, coughing a bit at the burn. Once I'd recovered, I slid the glass across to her. She filled it and slid it back.

"Right," I said, a bit hoarsely. "Okay, here it is. Am I making a huge mistake here?"

Alex fiddled with her glass, spinning it in her fingers. "About the heat contract? The fact that you're choosing to ask me makes it sound like you want someone to tell you yes."

I threw back the next shot—my fourth—wincing as it went down. "Cut me off after this next one, please," I said, pushing the glass toward her. She nodded and filled it. I sighed, trying to find the right words. "I don't think it's that. I mean, if I ask Jax or Flynn, they'll say they think it's a great idea to spend my heat together. If I ask Kam, he'll give me that sad-eyed smile and tell me it's my choice. At least if I ask you, you'll have an opinion that's not *full-steam-ahead*."

She nodded and knocked back another shot. A small furrow formed between her brows. Alex was dark-haired and sharp-featured — built like a cheetah, and with the same green-gold eyes. All of the fine lines around her eyes and mouth were unhappy ones.

"Would the situation be a lot simpler if my packmates hadn't fallen for you?" she said. "Yeah. It would be, for sure. In fact, if they weren't pining for you and Kameron like a pair of blushing schoolgirls nursing their first crushes, I'd probably tell you to go for it and enjoy the alpha horse cocks. No question about it — heat blockers suck and riding out an unfulfilled heat without blockers sucks even worse."

"But?" I prompted, feeling the alcohol begin to hit properly, loosening my muscles and probably my tongue.

She shrugged. "You already know. They're settling for a heat contract because you would have said no to anything more. That doesn't mean they don't still *want* more. And..." She gestured around, indicating not just the remote safehouse, but the entire situation. "... realistically, how would that even work right now?"

I saluted her with my shot glass and drained it. "That's what I said," I agreed around a cough.

"Here's the thing, though," Alex said. "The fact that my packmates are idiots doesn't change any of the rest of it. I've heard the horror stories. Unaccompanied heats are the worst. And Jax and Flynn may be idiots, but they're honorable idiots with really big dicks, who apparently know how to use them."

I choked on an unattractive snorting laugh, my hand flying to my mouth to cover it.

"If you're trying to argue on the *against* side, no offense, but you might want to brush up your debate skills a bit," I suggested.

She only shook her head and poured herself another shot. "Nah. See, as long as you've got it straight in your head, it's not your responsibility if a pair of alphas are thinking with their little brains instead of their big ones." She hesitated. "At least, as long as no fertile sperm get anywhere near fertile eggs."

I nodded solemnly, aware that I was finally reaching the stage of proper drunkenness. "A-fucking-men to that," I said.

"Honestly," Alex went on, "if you want objectivity, go talk to Beckett. He's been managing this kind of omega shit for longer than either of us have been alive… god alone knows how." The last few words were a low mutter.

"Huh," I said. "Y'know, that's a good idea. I'm shtill… *still* wrapping my brain around him being an omega. And *mated*. Shit."

I'd never had an older omega to help me navigate the minefield of estrus cycles and mate-bonds. My parents were both betas, and while I owed them my life and my freedom after the sacrifices they'd made to protect me from the Committee's tender mercies, they hadn't been much help with the nuts and bolts of my body and its responses. They'd tried, but... knowledge about alphomic biology was tightly regulated. You couldn't just run to the library and check out a book. They'd pretty much all been burned decades ago, back at the beginning of the Purge.

"I'll do that," I decided. "But maybe not till I sober up."

Alex snorted in amusement, her steady parade of downed shots finally starting to outpace alpha alcohol tolerance.

"I'm gonna do this," I told my empty shot glass. "I mean, since you're not dead shet... *set*... against it or anything."

"Not dead set against it, no," she said.

I studied her, taking in her straight spine and tight shoulders, even after eight shots, or nine, or whatever it had been. "Do you ever..." I made vague, waving motions with my fingers. "Like, at all anymore?"

She blinked at me without comprehension.

"Sex," I clarified, confirming that I'd reached the *brain-to-mouth filter failure* stage of drunkenness. "Do you ever have sex, since Irina died?"

"Oh." She poured yet another shot and drank it. "I mean... yeah. Not often, but when the circumstances line up, sure."

I frowned. "With omegas?" I asked, because she'd seemed, like, *really* against that idea after talking about how she'd lost her omega mate and pups.

But she shook her head quickly. "No, with beta men. No uteruses, see? They're safe, and usually okay with one-night stands."

My frown didn't smooth. "Beta men? You enjoy that? Really?"

Alex shrugged a shoulder. "I enjoy the ones who like to take a knot up the ass."

Comprehension dawned, and I made an exaggerated '*oh*' shape with my mouth. "Gotcha." I tapped the side of my nose. "I did that for Kam once, you know. With a..." I trailed off, trying to describe the shape of a dildo in the air. "Thingie. I think he got close — to coming, I mean — but he still couldn't get there."

Suddenly, this seemed like the saddest thing in the world. I met Alex's catlike green eyes, convinced that she would understand. I wasn't sure why, but I felt we'd connected somehow. It was different than the way I'd connected with Jax and Flynn. Less complicated in some ways. More complicated in others.

"He's got a huge crush on you," I confided. "He talked about how he'd like to tease your clit out of its sheath with his tongue and ride it all night long." I paused, remembering the night we'd spent exploring each other's bodies. "You should let him. He's got a really nice tongue."

Silence reigned for an uncomfortable beat.

Wait, had I really just said that out loud? Based on the perfectly blank expression on Alex's face, I had. It was *just* possible I should have stopped after four shots instead of five.

The alpha cleared her throat and gave the vodka bottle a long look—one that said she was thinking about foregoing the shot glass and going straight to the source. But the idea was stuck in my head now, and I couldn't let it go.

"No, listen though. If I'm doing this heat... thing, and you're going to be there to keep an eye on the others, you could, maybe... try to help Kam?" It was perfect. Why hadn't I thought of this before? "He's safe for you. He doesn't have a uterus anymore. And you're both so sad all the time. Maybe you could make each other less sad?"

Alex seemed to be holding her face very still. I couldn't tell what she was thinking, so I gave up and asked. "Well? What do you think?"

She blinked. "I... think we're both pretty drunk. Beckett should be back in a few hours with the contraceptives and other supplies. Maybe you should go sleep it off for a bit."

While I tried to interpret that with a brain that felt like it was slogging through molasses, she rose from the kitchen table and headed deeper into the house, taking the bottle with her. Once she'd disappeared, the ghost of Flynn's voice echoed in my head.

She didn't say no.

TWO

Leona

"BECKETT'S HERE." The clink of a glass being placed on a table accompanied Kam's matter-of-fact declaration.

I pried open gummy eyelids, unsure if I was hung over, still drunk, or some hellacious combination of both. "Great," I rasped, and reached for the water glass.

"I would make some comment about an omega doing vodka shots on an empty stomach…" he began, settling onto the overstuffed sectional couch that delineated two sides of the sunken nest in the safehouse's upstairs den.

"Yeah, don't bother," I told him. "Look at it this way—it's not like maintaining a professional demeanor is really that much of a necessity anymore."

Kam stretched, his rumpled white button-down shirt riding up, exposing a bit of olive skin below the side gusset. "We still don't know what Beckett's got in mind for us," he said. "You never know, maybe we'll have to give up all our vices."

He looked… *tired*. Not exactly a surprise. I was dealing with the shock of having to completely reinvent my life, and not knowing exactly what that would entail. By contrast, he already knew what was coming, at least in broad terms. He'd done this before.

His tousled dark hair, devoid of styling products, curled over his forehead. Bruised circles beneath his soulful brown eyes advertised his need for more uninterrupted sleep than he was currently getting.

We'd been here for a week. My heat was due to start in two days, but it could be a day early or late. Normally, I'd have taken my heat blocker last night, just in case. This time around, I hadn't. That still felt weird.

With luck, Beckett had been successful in getting the contraceptives he'd promised me—because apparently, the five of us were actually going to do this. Three alphas in our borrowed nest. The idea made me feel jittery. Not a bad sort of jittery, necessarily… though I would admit to a certain degree of fear of the unknown. When it came to being knotted by actual alphas, I was a thirty-one-year-old omega virgin.

I finished the glass of water Kam had brought me and set it down.

"Let me freshen up first, and then I'll go talk to him," I said. "Will you come with me?"

"Of course I will," Kam said. He rubbed his hands down his face, stretching the skin. "Tell me, though… how offended are you going to be if I curl up in a corner of the nest and sleep for four days straight while Jax and Flynn take turns fucking you?"

I tossed a pillow at his head. He batted it away with an amused snort.

After splashing cold water on my face in the ridiculous bathroom with its massive sunken tub and separate two-person shower, I gathered my disastrous hair into a bun and secured it with a couple of pencils that I'd liberated from downstairs. While my clothing was no longer limited to oversized T-shirts borrowed from the alphas, my available wardrobe was still painfully basic. The white tank top and black leggings I'd napped in would have to do.

Thankfully, our situation wasn't quite as dire as I'd originally assumed it was. I'd been taken from my loft in a three a.m. raid, and quite literally had nothing left to my name. But Jax and Flynn had managed to scoop Kam up from his apartment before the authorities started snooping around my closest contacts. He'd had time to grab his emergency bag, along with the ten thousand dollars in cash that he'd kept hidden in a wall safe.

I'd had a similar stash prepped and ready to go, for all the good it did me in the end. But—just as I would have shared my resources with Kam, had our positions been reversed—the money he'd hidden away was for both of us. If we were careful, it would be enough to sneak out of the country and make it to Jamaica, where my parents could help us set up new lives.

But now, while that might in fact be the safer option, it appeared we wouldn't be doing it. That was one of the things we needed to talk to Beckett about today, before my oncoming heat stole my higher brain functioning.

I headed back to the den and nudged Kam awake from his doze, trying not to feel guilty about doing so. Together, we trudged downstairs. Interesting smells wafted from the kitchen, making my stomach rumble.

I seemed to be hungry all the time, these last few days. At first, I'd assumed it was stress eating—not helped by the fact that the alphas always seemed to be shoving food at me. Eventually, I realized that it was my body bolstering its reserves for my upcoming heat. For several days, I would survive on only whatever water the others could get me to drink between peaks, burning fat for calories as my body shifted all its resources to my reproductive system.

Led by the nose, I followed the smells and found Jax standing over the electric stove. Flynn sat at the kitchen table, cutting a pile of fruit into pieces and dumping it in a big ceramic bowl. They both looked up as we entered. Flynn's face lit up; Jax flashed us a pleasant smile.

"Hey," Flynn said. "We're just stocking up. No one wants to cook after a good heat, but everyone wants to eat."

I nodded in understanding. "What is that?" I asked Jax, inhaling the scent of meat and browned potatoes.

"Shepherd's pie," he said. "Well, cottage pie, I guess, since it's beef and not lamb. Try some?"

I crossed to him as though drawn to his side by a length of silken cord. The pie itself was in the oven, baking to a lovely golden brown. He scraped the contents of one bowl into another bowl and handed it to me—mashed potatoes sitting on top of a mixture of cooked ground beef and diced vegetables. I took the spoon he offered and devoured it like a starving coyote.

At the table, Flynn chuckled. "Come here for a minute when you're done."

While I was distracted, he'd foisted an apple on Kam, who bit into it with a crunch. I scraped up the last couple of bites of deconstructed cottage pie and offered Jax a tentative smile of thanks before rinsing the bowl and spoon in the sink. I approached Flynn cautiously. He set the knife down and hooked me close to him with a gentle hand at the back of my neck.

My heart rabbited, my body unused to that kind of casual touch from an alpha. When he buried his nose at the base of my neck and shoulder and breathed in, gooseflesh erupted across my entire body. He let me go, holding the breath he'd just taken like a wine connoisseur assessing a rare vintage.

"You're gonna be early," he said. "Go talk to Beckett now and get that out of the way. I want to have plenty of time to play before we need to get down to business."

I couldn't suppress a shiver. Kam's eyes on me were soft when I turned to him.

"Come on," he said. "Let's go make sure everything's in order."

Nodding wordlessly, I followed him with Flynn's call of, "Don't worry—I'm gonna play with you, too, Ginger Tea!" chasing us out.

"Why do I feel like we're on the menu every bit as much as the cottage pie and fruit salad?" I murmured.

"Because we are," Kam said wryly. "Well, you are, anyway. That's basically what you're signing up for, you realize."

I hadn't realized—not properly. Not until just now. My hazy memories from last time involved the alphas holding back, respecting boundaries that I'd needed for my own safety, but hadn't *wanted* in the desperation of the moment. Now, I was extending them carte blanche, at least within the framework of what we'd all agreed to ahead of time.

"I have absolutely no idea what I'm getting into, do I?" I asked.

Kam huffed in what was probably amusement. "You're about to spend four solid days riding a sex-high." He hesitated. "And I'm apparently going to be caught inside the blast zone for most of it. Should be interesting, if nothing else."

I stepped in front of him and turned to face him with my hand on his arm, stopping us in the hallway. "You *are* okay with this, right?" I asked, feeling a wash of guilt over my drunken confession to Alex earlier.

"Yes, *odama*," he said gently. "I'm okay with the nice alphas eating us for breakfast. We're here, we're safe—for a given definition of the word—and it makes no sense for you to take that toxic poison you call a heat blocker when you can have a natural heat shared with alphas you genuinely like. I like them, too, by the way. In case that wasn't obvious."

I knew he was telling the truth. I also knew he didn't really think he'd be able to get anything out of it beyond that—not after the mutilation he'd undergone as an adolescent. That was clear in his tone, even if he hadn't meant for it to come through.

"I... might have confessed to Alex that you have a crush on her while I was drunk," I blurted, wincing before adding, "and asked her to have sex with you."

Kam's face went utterly still. Sheepishly, I let my hand drop from his arm.

"At which point she freaked out and ran for the hills, I assume?" he asked slowly.

I sighed. "Not exactly. She, uh, changed the subject." *And then ran for the hills with a bottle of vodka in tow*, I didn't add.

He sighed, too. "You probably shouldn't have done that."

"I know," I told him. "And I'm sorry. But she's sad, and miserable, and she's going to try to wall herself off from what's happening for four straight days while the house is choked with heat pheromones. And you're also sad, and miserable, and you're going to try to wall yourself off from what's happening the minute I'm too out of things to stop you. I just want you to be happy, Kam." I studied his tired, beautiful face. "If she offered, would you turn her down?"

"No," he said. "I wouldn't. That's what scares me."

I cupped his cheek in my palm. "Promise me you'll try to enjoy yourself, whether it's with her, or with Flynn, or even Jax. Maybe it will be different with my heat pheromones and the alpha pheromones together."

I could see in his eyes that he still thought it was hopeless. His beta owners had considered him too difficult to deal with; too stubborn for use in the breeding pens despite his impeccable purebred bloodlines. They'd sterilized him before tossing him into the slave market—ripping out his ovotestes and his womb, suturing his birthing passage closed. We'd tried before, but in the end, we hadn't been able to work around what had been done to his body.

Despite his obvious discomfort with the subject, he covered my hand with his and slid it forward so he could press a kiss to my palm. "If it makes you feel better, I don't think I'm going to have much say in the matter if Flynn gets his way. I'm sure I'll enjoy myself to whatever degree I still can."

I had the feeling he was humoring me, the same way he'd been humoring me when he swore that our failed sex experiment the night before my capture had been '*fine.*' But it would be churlish to press the issue any further.

"Okay," I said. "I'm holding you to that."

He found a smile for me. We continued to the living room, where Beckett had set up his makeshift office. He was waiting for us there, a brown paper bag sitting on one corner of the coffee table.

"Hello," he greeted. "It's last minute, but I was able to acquire everything you need. Still comfortable with your choice, I hope?"

"Committed, anyway," I replied. "I've got a bit too much of a crawling-out-of-my-own-skin thing going on for the word comfortable to feel appropriate."

He nodded, unperturbed. "You're getting close, it seems. If you're ready, I can administer the contraceptive shot for you now. There's probably no point in putting it off."

I swallowed and nodded agreement, watching as he drew a sealed syringe and an unlabeled vial from the bag. He tore open the syringe's plastic packaging and plunged the needle through the vial's rubber seal, drawing up its contents. After flicking the syringe to loosen the air bubbles, he pressed the plunger until a bead of liquid dripped from the needle tip. Then, he turned to me.

"This will prevent ovulation," he said. "Normally you'd release an egg with every peak. With this stuff in your system, you won't. There's also a selection of condoms, along with three sizes of cervical caps. You'll need to try them ahead of time to see which size is most comfortable and secure, but as an omega who's never been pregnant, I would guess the medium size is your best bet."

Kam had been standing nearby, watching the exchange. "You know," he said with a hint of wry humor, "it's a bit surreal watching you dispense information on cervical caps when I've also seen you wearing a balaclava and waving an Uzi around."

"It was an AK-47," Beckett said placidly, and Kam gave a little snort.

"Well, I for one am grateful for both of your skill sets," I told him. With a gesture, I indicated the syringe. "Is that going in my shoulder?"

"It's intramuscular, yes," he said. "Your shoulder will be fine. Left arm?"

I nodded and offered him my left shoulder, bared by the tank top. He steadied my arm and a moment later I felt the pinch of the needle entering. A few seconds later, it was done. Maybe I should have had more misgivings about letting this person I barely knew inject drugs into my body… but he'd saved us twice. He was the one and only reason I wasn't currently awaiting a show trial followed by a messy execution at the hands of Enoch Sloane.

Also, there was the small matter that I'd been using drugs provided by people I barely knew to control my omega biology since I was sixteen.

"Thank you," I told him. "And not just for the shot."

Beckett gave me the same small, tight smile that I'd seen several times before. It was a smile that said he appreciated the sentiment, while also hating the reasons behind it. I wondered how long he'd been fighting as part of the underground, and how he dealt with the frustration of things never changing, except for the worse.

"Don't mention it," he said.

I'd been poised to ask him the same question I'd asked Alex—*am I making a mistake?* But somehow, that wasn't the question I needed answered anymore.

"Is there anything you think I should know, going into this?" I asked instead. "My parents were betas, and I've been suppressing my heats for fifteen years. I'm going in blind; I have no idea what I'm doing."

Kam's hand found mine, our fingers tangling as he gave me a supportive squeeze. I squeezed back.

Beckett leaned back on the couch. "The first rule of a heat contract is to choose your alphas wisely. You've done that already. As much as I hate to say it, beyond that, hormones will pretty much dictate that you'll take whatever they dish out, and probably beg for more. Hence the importance of rule number one."

I thought back to my vague memories of Romania—of begging for sex barely an hour after I'd explicitly refused it, a slave to my own desperation.

"Point taken," I said.

But he shook his head. "Don't take that the wrong way. You've chosen three honorable alphas, one of whom will be on guard the whole time to make sure no one gets carried away. Your heat should be a time of joyful connection. Sharing it with packmates and friends is a blessing. Cherish it."

My throat tightened, and I had to swallow against the thickness there. I gave him a nod of understanding in lieu of words. In a perfect world, I would be the sort of omega who wanted pups, living in a world where that dream posed no danger. Kam and I would be mated to a pack of alphas, sharing my heat joyously and without reservations.

Failing that—living in the world we inhabited now—this heat contract might be the only taste of that kind of happiness I would ever get.

Kam shifted beside me. "I understand that this is a sensitive question you may not be able to answer, but do you ever get to share heats with your mate?"

Beckett's answering smile was achingly sad. "Not nearly as often as we'd like," he said.

"That's how I learned to cherish the times we do have."

THREE

Leona

THAT EVENING, I explored the wonderful world of cervical caps and confirmed that I was, in fact, a size medium. I also confirmed that the things were awkward as hell to put in and take out.

"Stop laughing," I growled at Kam. "If I'm too heat-drunk to deal with getting it in and out, you're going to be first up to pinch hit."

That at least shut him up.

I was growing restless, the same feeling of my skin being too tight and hot that I remembered from my last heat. Flynn had been right. I wasn't going to last two days. This was happening tomorrow, and there was no stopping it now.

The nest wasn't right. I rearranged it, then rearranged it again half an hour later. Finally, Kam coaxed me into the comically large sunken bathtub, with its endless supply of on-demand hot water. I fidgeted in his arms, both wanting the feel of skin on skin and finding myself frustrated by it.

A knock sounded at the door of the den, muffled through the closed connecting door to the bathroom. "I'll take care of it," Kam said, hoisting his lean body out of the bath and wrapping a towel around his hips.

A couple of minutes later he returned, poking his head in. "Jax brought food."

I wrinkled my nose, unsure if I wanted it or not.

"There's chocolate cake," he added.

My stomach growled like a horny alpha in response to those three magic words, the fickle little bitch. "Coming," I said, and hauled my traitorous body out of the warm water.

Clad in one of Flynn's black T-shirts, I padded in and found a plate waiting for me with a slice of the cottage pie sending up curls of steam—presumably reheated, unless Jax had whipped up a second one after we left. A wedge salad joined it on one corner of the plate. The promised slab of chocolate cake sat in a separate, smaller dessert dish, with a scoop of vanilla ice cream melting over it.

Kam was already tucking into his food, still wearing nothing but the towel because why the hell not? I settled in diagonally across from him on the overstuffed sectional and dove in.

Yes, I started with the cake. *So sue me.*

"Jax asked if they could come to the nest around ten tomorrow morning," Kam said, once the initial round of face stuffing had eased. "I told him it was fine. Is that all right?"

I hesitated, then nodded. "I think that'll be about right, to be honest."

"He also said Beckett will be heading out to meet with some other people about what comes afterward. Even though he's on pheromone suppressors, he didn't think you'd appreciate a strange omega rattling around the place while you're in heat."

I gave a humorless little laugh. "He'd know better than me—I've got no clue. And *crap*. I totally intended to grill him about the what-comes-next part when we saw him earlier."

"He may not know yet, if he's still hashing things out with other members of the underground," Kam said. "I'm willing to bet the whole thing's organized in cells. Good for security, in case someone important gets captured. Not so good for quick communication with the higher-ups."

I grunted. "You're probably right. Not like I'll be in a position to fret about it for the next few days."

"I expect you'll be in a bunch of different positions, but probably not that one, true. Don't worry. I can fret for both of us," Kam replied wryly.

I wrinkled my nose at him. After eating a bit of my salad and maybe three-quarters of the cottage pie, I pushed the rest away. Kam divided his cake in half with his fork and pushed one of the pieces into my dessert dish.

"I love you," I told him.

"I know," he said, and reached for my unfinished salad and entrée.

When everything was gone, he took the plates and silverware downstairs to wash. I let him, figuring I wasn't really fit for company tonight. At least, not for company that wasn't him. Since there was really nothing else that needed to be done, I grabbed *The Unbearable Lightness of Being* from the corner table and dragged it down into the nest with me to read. Cocooned in two fuzzy blankets and propped on a small mountain of pillows, I made it through about nine pages before I fell asleep.

———◆———

When I woke up, my skin felt hot and prickly. I remembered this feeling from before, and the bad associations made my heart speed up until it was thudding wildly against my chest.

"Good morning," Kam said. "It's almost nine-thirty. The alphas will be here in about half an hour. How are you feeling?"

I blinked gritty eyelids open, revealing our cozy nest lit by soft red bulbs. I couldn't help but compare my surroundings to my untimely heat where we'd been held captive in the cave and at risk of discovery at any moment. Aside from the obvious upgrade in comfort and luxury, this felt *safe*.

I was grateful to be in a remote house where no one would be able to find us. My packmate extended a glass of orange juice in my direction, and the earlier adrenaline spike subsided to a generalized feeling of shakiness.

I wriggled out of soft blankets that suddenly felt as irritating as burlap and took the glass from him.

"Umm," I rasped. "Not great? It's definitely coming on soon."

The orange juice tasted off, like my taste buds were screwed up or something. I drank it anyway.

Kam gave me a sympathetic nod. "Your scent's starting to change. If you want a shower, you should probably have it now. I've already had one. I even left you some hot water."

"It's a tankless heater," I pointed out.

"Like I said, I left you some," Kam said, and took the half-finished glass of juice when I handed it back.

I stuck my tongue out at him, but I did stagger upright and shuffle off to the bathroom. In the end, I settled on a lukewarm shower as being the least irritating option. Hot water made my already feverish head swim. Cool water made my nerves feel like someone was running sandpaper over them. I gave myself a cursory wash and kept my hair as dry as I could. The idea that someone might wash it for me later sent an unexpected jolt through my belly, and a pulse of slick dribbled down my leg.

O-*kay*, then.

I turned off the water and dried myself with one of the fluffy towels from the rack. Kam had left a fresh oversized T-shirt on the vanity for me. Well… maybe *fresh* wasn't the word. It was worn to gossamer softness from repeated use, almost translucent in places, and it smelled like sitting in the woods with a steaming cup of mulled cider. With a jolt, I realized that Flynn and Jax had taken turns wearing this shirt without washing it in between.

Holy. Shit.

I buried my nose in the fabric and breathed in. I might as well have been snorting a line of coke. Eventually, I emerged from my pheromone high enough to pull it over my head. Even the well-worn cotton irritated me, but the scent made up for it. And while it might have been perfectly acceptable etiquette to welcome your heat partners into the nest while buck naked for all I knew, I wasn't *quite* there yet.

My hands trembled a bit as I filled the cervical cap with spermicide and put it in, cursing under my breath the whole time. When it was finally in place, I straightened and moved to stand in front of the mirror, looking at my reflection as though it belonged to a stranger.

Flushed cheeks. Parted lips. Dilated pupils. Nipples threatening to drill holes through the ancient T-shirt. A cloud of *eau de desperation* forming an almost tangible aura around me as my body pumped out its honey-flavored perfume.

Welp. As Kam had said, this was going to be… interesting.

I let myself out of the bathroom and immediately walked into a wall of alpha pheromones. They were already here. Three sets of eyes fell on me as though drawn by a magnet.

"Hi," I said nervously, trying to ignore the fact that I wasn't wearing underwear and I'd just dribbled out another pulse of slick. Flynn's nostrils flared.

"Hello," Jax said, his gaze dipping to the hem of the borrowed shirt.

Alex was the first to tear her eyes away. "We're just getting everything in place. But I can finish up with that. Make yourself comfortable, and you can hash out any final details. Beckett's gone, by the way. We've got the place to ourselves."

The melding of delicious alpha scents in the air was threatening to steal my higher brain functions right there and then. I unstuck my feet from the floor and descended into the sunken nest area, wading through fur and cushions. Wanting the feel of all of that softness around me, I sunk down next to where Kam was sitting primly on the sectional, pressing my shoulder against his knee.

He rested a hand on the back of my neck to soothe me. His thumb rubbed gently across the sensitive skin as I drank in his reassuring presence.

Jax and Flynn entered the nest and sank down across from me — Flynn lowering himself smoothly into a cross-legged position. Jax moved more slowly, still favoring his left side after the muscle damage he'd suffered from an experimental nerve agent.

"We're gonna take care of you," Flynn said, his voice a low basso rumble. "Both of you. But Jax wants to ask you first if there's stuff you particularly like or don't like."

I raised an eyebrow, struggling to hold onto rational thought beneath the onslaught of pheromones. "Just Jax? Not you?" I asked.

Flynn grinned at me. "Nah. I've got a pretty good idea already. I was doing more than sitting in the corner jacking off last time, you know."

A full-body shiver took me, as hazy memories of Flynn's rough voice narrating filthy suggestions as Kam fucked me with a dildo flitted across my mind. He'd been watching us the whole time, cataloguing my responses. Probably Kam's as well, now that I thought about it.

"Oh," I managed.

Jax shot Flynn a flat stare before turning his attention back to me. "Unlike my packmate, I'm not a mind reader. I'd love to hear about your likes and dislikes, so we can make sure this is as good for you as it can possibly be."

I looked at him blankly for long moments, trying not to get swept up in the way his full lips moved as he spoke, or how incredibly blue his eyes were.

"Uhh…" Outside of my last heat, the sum total of my experience consisted of the times Kam and I had fooled around. "I like… oral?"

"Giving and receiving?" Jax asked. "Or just receiving?"

"Both," I said, aware that an alpha cock was likely to be a much different proposition than Kam's slender, half-hard shaft. The idea still made my mouth water. I swallowed and licked my lips, both alphas' gazes dipping to my mouth as I did.

I thought about the stories betas told about alphas, and added reluctantly, "I don't think I want it rough. I wouldn't want to be held down or… forced."

Kam's fingers stilled against the skin of my neck. I glanced up at him, but his face was a mask.

"Our sweet girl wants to be worshipped," Flynn said. "I could've told you that. It's our Ginger Tea here who wants to be pinned down by the throat and used over and over until he breaks."

The faintest sound of an inhaled breath came from above me, and my eyes flew to Kam's face again. He was still holding his expression carefully neutral, but his eyes had darkened, and there was a fine tremor in his hand.

Jax looked between his packmate and mine before addressing Kam in a wry tone. "I think we'll start out concentrating on Leona. If this asshole is wrong about things, just stay near Alex and she'll make sure he minds his manners. And if he's right, well... we'll have plenty of time to play with that, once the initial edge is off."

"I'll take that under consideration," Kam replied, a bit hoarsely.

Flynn let out a rumble of laughter.

I frowned up at my packmate, placing a hand on his knee and giving it a squeeze. "Are you all right, *odama*?"

The atmosphere had grown a bit... *odd*, and I couldn't quite pin it down. I felt like Flynn's words should have upset me, rather than sending a trickle of heat down my spine. There was nothing threatening in his scent or demeanor. If anything, it felt *fond*. And Kam didn't seem upset, as such... only disconcerted.

"Of course I am, Leo," he said. "Let's just keep the focus on you, where it belongs."

"I'm good at multitasking," Flynn said serenely. "But that's enough talk. As much as I like seeing you in my shirt, I'd much rather see you out of it. Easier to give you a massage that way."

My breath caught at the idea of Flynn's big hands running over my body. I felt a flush heat my cheeks. "I'm not sure that's..." I trailed off, unsure how to finish the sentence.

"Do as he says," Jax ordered. There was nothing unkind in his tone, but the hint of alpha power beneath it went straight to my core. "Alex is watching over things. Your *odama* is watching over things. It's time to let go and let the rest of us take care of you."

I couldn't breathe for a moment, as a lifetime of struggle not to succumb to omega weakness battled my body's need for surrender to the alphas who would knot me through my heat. My gaze flew to Kam's. He took my chin in his slender fingers and leaned down, pressing a kiss to my lips.

"I'm right here, beloved," he murmured into our shared air. "But it's them you need right now."

Liquid warmth rolled through my body. The nest was awash in the scents of cypress and musk, cardamom and sandalwood. It felt like a drug… like an answer to a question I hadn't thought to ask yet.

"Come to us, Leona," Flynn rumbled.

Without conscious thought, my arms and legs moved, pulled by that tone of casual command. I crawled toward the alphas who'd shepherded me through a heat once before, the softness of the nest cushioning my hands and knees. When I reached them, I knelt, not able to look either of them in the eye.

A dark-skinned hand entered my field of vision. Fingers cupped my jaw, and Flynn's thumb brushed over my lower lip, lighting every nerve in my body. My nipples tightened into painful points. He lifted my chin until I had to look at him.

"Shirt off, little omega," he said. The merest hint of an alpha bark had me scrambling to pull the oversized tee over my head and toss it away. I crossed my arms over my chest to cover it, not even sure where the impulse had come from. My sex was throbbing.

"None of that," Jax said gently. "Let go, Leona. We've got you now."

A touch on the side of my neck guided me to bare my throat for them, and my whole body followed a moment later. I rolled onto my back among the soft furs and cushions, all of the tension flowing out of me as I showed the alphas my belly, and nothing horrible happened.

"So beautiful," Flynn said, running a single fingertip from my chin, down my throat, between my breasts, and along my stomach to my navel.

I shivered, feeling more slick gathering between my legs, and let the alphas take control.

FOUR

Leona

I COULD HAVE everything I wanted this time, I thought distantly. *This was allowed.* There would be no holding back, no poor substitutes for what I really needed.

"Lie on your front," Flynn said, urging me to roll over with a touch. "Not that I wasn't enjoying the view."

I did as I was bid, humming a bit as I nestled into all the softness. Jax shifted position to settle next to my head, which lay cradled on my arms. A moment later, callused fingers threaded through my hair, dragging across my scalp over and over in a soothing, rhythmic motion.

"That's more like it," Flynn said.

Something clicked above me, and I shivered as cool wetness dribbled down my spine. The click came again — the opening and closing of a bottle cap. Strong hands slid up and down the length of my back, spreading the massage oil over the feverish flesh. I groaned as thumbs pressed into the tight muscles between my shoulder blades, knotted by months... *years...* of unrelenting tension.

One by one, the knots gave way, as though they were as powerless beneath an alpha's hands as the rest of me was. Bliss and need grew in equal measure as Flynn dug into my muscles while Jax's fingers stroked and tugged at my scalp.

"You like that?" Flynn asked, a purr rumbling up in his chest.

"Yes, alphas," I replied breathlessly. "Please don't stop."

"We're not gonna stop, sweet thing," Flynn said.

This wasn't full heat yet—not even close. But the promise behind the words still made my empty passage clench.

Flynn's strong hands moved lower, kneading my ass. I squirmed, my legs falling open invitingly as I proceeded at maximum velocity toward full-on omega slut mode. Instead of taking the invitation, though, he chuckled and continued down my legs, kneading my hamstrings and calves, and finally my bare feet. A tiny squeak escaped me as his thumbs dug into my arches—the kind of noise prey makes when it's been caught.

When he worked his way back up my legs, his big hands roamed the insides of my thighs. Anticipation froze my breath in my lungs. He paused, chuckling again.

"Might want to keep breathing, sweet girl," he said. "It's kind of important, after all."

His fingertips teased the final inch separating him from where I wanted him. My lungs burned, lightheadedness making me dizzy until the air finally exploded free in a gush, and I dragged in panting breaths.

"There you go," Flynn said, and slid several thick fingers inside of me.

I keened at the perfect, burning stretch of it, and tried to fuck back against him, driving them deeper.

"Shh," Jax murmured. His fingers tangled in my thick hair, wrapping it around and around his hand until the strands tugged against my scalp, holding me in place. "Stay still, Leona. Just let it happen."

I trembled, desperate for more, more, *more* as Flynn slowly thrust his fingers in and out of my body.

"So wet already," Flynn said, "and you're not even near your first peak yet."

His fingers trailed farther forward to circle my clit. I grabbed fistfuls of the fur beneath me, feeling my release building. Flynn alternated fucking my passage and teasing my clit, driving me a little bit higher each time, until the pressure finally became too much and escaped its confines in a series of wrenching spasms.

I moaned, going completely limp as my muscles unclenched. The hand in my hair eased. I peeled my eyes open in time to see Jax pulling his shirt over his head. He tugged the waistband of his dark track pants down far enough to free his cock. It was hard, and seemed very, *very* large all of the sudden.

"Bet you're glad that shit they pumped into you in Romania didn't break your dick, huh?" Flynn asked.

Jax shot him an unamused look. "Yes, thank you. I'm glad it didn't break my dick, asshole."

Personally, I was having trouble focusing on anything but the alpha horse cock on display. Despite the orgasm that had just floored me—*literally*—fresh hunger was already coiling in my gut. I wanted that cock, and this time, I was going to have it, damn it. I elbow-crawled halfway onto Jax's lap, looking up at him from under my lashes.

"Hello, beautiful," he said, gathering my hair back again. "See something you want, I take it?"

I smiled at him, giddy with how different this was from last time. With how *perfect* it was. "Yes, alpha," I said breathlessly, and reveled in the feel of his big hand guiding my lips to him.

I'd been right. It was nothing like taking Kam in my mouth. I licked the salty head, dragging my lips around and over the blunt tip until the hand in my hair pressed me down. I had to stretch my lips wide around Jax's girth, and a moan vibrated up from my throat.

"Ooh. That looks awfully good, sweet thing," Flynn said from behind me. Without warning, his fingers breached me again. "Think she'll bite you if I make her come again while you're fucking her mouth, Jax?"

I whined as his fingers curled, stretching me from the inside with every slow stroke in and out. More slick dribbled out of me, the wetness making tiny, obscene sucking noises as he moved.

"No," Jax said dismissively. "Of course she won't. She's a good girl." His hand urged me to take him deeper, even as Flynn twisted his wrist and teased my clit with the barest brushes of his thumb.

I rocked between them. Getting away from one only meant pushing the other deeper. My muscles trembled with the desire to *take, take, take.* I wanted to take everything they had, over and over—until the growing void inside me was full to overflowing, and they were empty and sated, tied to me irrevocably.

The teasing brushes against my clit gained purpose, demanding that my body respond. And it did—helpless before the power of pheromones and my own need. My second climax swallowed me like a bottomless pit opening up beneath me, and I cried out around the cock in my mouth. Neither alpha let up, Flynn's fingers drawing more and more from me until I couldn't tell down from up, and my vision dimmed to gray.

When awareness returned, it was clear that some time had passed. I'd been moved, and was lying sprawled on the weird, curvy divan thing with my head and shoulders supported on a familiar lap, and a blond head buried between my thighs.

"*Mmph*," I whimpered, as Jax's tongue lapped lazily along my slit. Tingles of sensation darted along my spine like champagne bubbles.

"Always knew she'd be responsive as hell," Flynn observed from somewhere nearby. Callused fingers tweaked my left nipple, tugging it up until it slid free, my breast bouncing.

"Hello. You all right, *odama*?" Kam asked.

His slender fingers stroked the hair back from my face, and I hummed, my body thrumming with a strange combination of need and relaxation.

"Mm-hmm," I managed, licking my lips and craning to look up at him with hazy eyes. "You were right. This weird sex-couch thing makes more sense with two people."

I was slurring my words a bit.

I didn't care.

This was awesome.

The thing I was lying on looked like some crazy piece of modern art. I'd tried it out shortly after we'd arrived and declared it not remotely comfortable for reading, at which point Kam had chuckled at me and explained that it was sex furniture. Now, with my ass supported on one curved end at exactly the right height for Jax to kneel between my legs, I was a convert.

"It's great. Exactly the right shape to support a sexually exhausted omega so we can sexually exhaust her some more," Flynn agreed. "So, is it working?"

He tweaked my nipple again at the same moment Jax's tongue dragged over my clit. My eyes rolled back. "*Nngh*," I told him.

"I think it's working," Kam said, sounding a bit breathless.

I made uncoordinated grabby-hands motions toward Flynn. He leaned down until I could bury my nose against the base of his throat and inhale his thick, spicy scent. A purr rose in his chest. He let me nuzzle at him for a bit while Jax continued to lick me toward another peak, but eventually he tilted my head back and brushed his lips over mine in a teasing kiss that grew gradually more heated until I was desperate for air... but not quite desperate enough to pull away.

It went on and on—lips and tongues and nipping teeth, until Jax closed his lips around my clit and sucked. I arched and came silently, pinned between two mouths. Something inside me felt like it had broken open, spilling out fresh need at the same time my body gushed a new pulse of slick onto Jax's face. He lapped it up with a pleased rumble that vibrated against my oversensitive flesh, and I shuddered in Kam's arms.

Flynn ended the kiss with a final sharp nip to my lower lip. I panted, staring at Kam's upside down face above me. Flynn took Kam's jaw in his large hand and tilted his face up.

"You're perfuming," he said, shifting his grip to cup Kam's nape and roll his head to the side, baring his throat.

"Yes," Kam replied faintly, as Flynn lowered his nose to the bare skin of Kam's neck and breathed in deeply.

"Mmm," said Flynn. "There's my ginger tea and lemon. We're gonna have such fun with you later…"

Kam shivered, and I felt a twitch beneath me as his omega cock tried to harden. I writhed my upper body sinuously in his lap, and his arms tightened around me convulsively.

"Yes, alpha," he whispered.

The emptiness inside me was growing again, despite the orgasms. It was becoming unpleasant now—all the touching and licking and kissing more of a tease than a relief. I whimpered, feeling the urge to turn over and present.

"It's time, Leona," Jax said, pressing a lingering kiss to my mons.

Kam gave me a final squeeze and let me go. Jax helped me slither down to the soft interior of the nest, where I rolled over onto my elbows and knees. My lower back arched in response to the rough fingertips sliding along the length of my spine. The room felt hot and close.

"Please, alphas," I begged, knowing that this time, I could have what I wanted. "Please fill me up—I'm so empty…"

"We've got you, sweet thing," Flynn said from somewhere behind me. I heard the rustle of fabric and craned around, needing to see. I was rewarded with the sight of a hot, naked alpha, his rich brown skin gleaming in the warm light of the nest. He ripped open a small packet and rolled the latex sheath over his straining cock.

Jax settled in front of me, and I turned to look at him. He was bare from the waist up, but still wore his loose track pants. Kam had retreated to the sectional. His eyes met mine and held for a long moment, until the third alpha in the room drew my attention. Alex sat on the other side of the couch, watching me with a gaze sharp as a hawk's.

I was still looking at her when big hands clasped my hips from behind. I closed my eyes, imagining how Flynn's dark skin would look pressed against my pale body, and let out a shaky breath.

"Gonna fill you up so good, sweet thing," Flynn rumbled.

Another whimper escaped as something impossibly large and unyielding slid against my soaked folds, lining up with my passage and pressing in with steady insistence. My body stretched to accommodate Flynn's girth with a delicious burn unlike anything I'd ever felt before.

I cried out, tears gathering in my eyes, and Jax's thumb swiped them away when they overflowed.

"You're doing so well for us," he said. "Such a good omega, taking Flynn's cock. We're going to make you feel so good."

More tears spilled over, and a sob caught in my throat as Flynn's huge erection filled me. I felt as though I had been made entirely for this moment, and it had taken me thirty-one years to get here.

"Please," I whispered. "Please, please, *please*—"

He began to move, and I was lost. Thought fled, leaving only instinct behind. It was too much, and not enough. It was *everything*. The world beyond the place where our bodies joined faded to unimportance. It could have lasted minutes or hours—I had no idea. I was drowning in scent, awash in emotion and touch and sensation.

Jax's thumb brushed my lower lip and pressed inside, sliding past my teeth, over my tongue. Flynn's hips snapped against mine, jolting my body with every thrust, a low growl rumbling in his throat. One of his big hands released his grip on my waist, sliding up my back to close possessively over the mating gland at the juncture of my neck and shoulder.

I screamed, my body clamping around Flynn's cock. He went still for an endless moment, then jerked through his release with a deep groan. I felt him panting behind me, even as the knot at the base of his cock swelled, locking us together and stretching me even further.

"God, Leona," he said hoarsely.

"Look at you two," Jax murmured, stroking my tearstained face with the backs of his fingers. "Come on, love. Let's get you curled up on your side so you can rest and enjoy your knot. Alex and I will watch the nest for you."

"Kam?" I rasped, as Jax helped Flynn maneuver us onto our sides with as little jostling as possible. Even so, Flynn's knot shifted inside me, and I shuddered in fresh ecstasy.

A slender figure knelt in front of me as I settled in, spooned from behind by Flynn's bulk. "I'm here, *odama*."

I reached for him and he came to me, bracketing me from the front. Now that the peak had broken, the sweat cooling on my skin lent a faint chill to my body—but Jax laid a blanket over us, and with an alpha at my back and my *odama* at my front, there was enough heat to chase it away. I floated in a blissful, trancelike state while Flynn stroked my hair and murmured endearments in my ear, until eventually my body released its hold on him.

Flynn eased out of me as gently as he could, and he and Kam held me pressed between them. Temporarily sated, I drifted into sleep.

FIVE

Kameron

FLYNN GOT UP and disposed of the condom once he was sure Leo was down for the count, but as soon as he and Jax had cleaned her up to their satisfaction, he returned to his place curled around her back.

She was totally out of it by that point, not even stirring when I carefully extricated myself from her arms and returned to my perch on one end of the sectional couch. I was a wreck, and I didn't know what to do about it—my phantom nipples aching, my cock pulsing and oversensitive against the seam of my jeans.

This time around, even I could smell the faint perfume my body was putting out in response to all the heat pheromones choking the room. Jax came and crouched in front of me. Part of me wanted to cringe back from him, and the other part wanted to fall forward into his arms and beg him to take care of me. I did neither.

"You don't look like an omega who's enjoying himself in the heat-nest," Jax said without judgment. "What can I do to help?"

"I'm fine," I said. "Everything's fine. I'm not the focus here."

If I became the focus, then I risked finding out once and for all that there was no hope for me. Right now, the possibility existed that I could still experience some sort of connection with these alphas, however stunted. But if I let them try and I still couldn't perform as an omega in the heat-nest should… it was over. How ironic that between Leo and myself, I'd always been the one with the big talk when it came to sex with alphas… but now that it was actually on offer, I was terrified.

"You're lying," Jax said, "but that's your prerogative. I respect your choice."

A new voice intruded. "I don't."

My eyes flew to Alex, curled on the other section of the couch like a jungle cat lounging on a rock.

"I won't have an omega huddled at the edge of the nest, looking like he wants to sink through the floor and disappear," she continued, tone steely. Her forest-colored alpha gaze fell on me with a weight so heavy it threatened to bow my shoulders. "Not on *my* pack's watch. Come here."

I swallowed convulsively, my heart rising in my throat.

"You tell 'im, Alex," Flynn said, not moving from his spot in the nest. "Soften him up a bit, and I'll be along to help in a few hours, after Leona wakes up."

Alex didn't even spare him a glance. That heavy gaze was still resting squarely on me. "You're not listening to your alpha," she said, in a deceptively soft voice. "Why is that?"

Her summons had been a command... but it was also a promise of protection. These alphas had protected us, even at the risk of their own lives. And god, how I wanted someone to protect me—even if it was from myself.

I bowed my head and slid to the cushion-covered floor. "I'm sorry, alpha."

"Don't be sorry," Alex said. "Just get your omega ass over here."

Jax looked between us, his blue eyes assessing my defeated posture. "Be careful with him, *alef.*"

"He doesn't want careful," Alex replied, still not looking at her packmate. "He wants someone to remind him of his value here. Of his place."

"What *is* my place here?" I whispered, my gaze wandering past Jax to fall on my *odama*, held securely in Flynn's arms as she slept off the aftermath of her first peak.

"Your place is to be given whatever you need while you're under our care," Alex said. "No matter what that might be."

My throat closed up and I crawled to her. She reached out a hand, and I followed the touch on my jaw as she positioned me on a pile of cushions heaped in front of her on the floor next to the couch.

"Right now, I'm pretty sure you need to stop thinking," she told me. Her voice turned wry. "Believe it or not, I'm familiar with that particular problem."

I gazed up at her, wondering what would be left of me if I let go of all the thoughts and worries swirling around the inside of my brain like angry dust devils. Those worries seemed to define me these days.

Alex was tall and strong and sharply beautiful—dark-haired and green-eyed and leanly muscled beneath the black tank top and gray sweatpants she wore. Her feet were bare.

She didn't crack a smile. Her expression might as well have belonged to a statue of Lady Justice, or maybe the Huntress Diana. I thought about the hotel in Bucharest, before everything had fallen apart—when I had waxed lyrical to Leo about teasing the enigmatic female alpha's clit from inside its folds with my tongue.

And... *god*. She knew about that little fantasy now, didn't she? Leo had blurted it out during a drunken confession. I should probably be angry about that, or maybe mortified. Shouldn't I?

Alex's long fingers tangled in my hair and tugged, the pull on my scalp landing just a hairsbreadth on the wrong side of pain. I gasped and arched my head back, my throat bare to her gaze as my cock throbbed and jerked weakly against my fly. Why the hell had I decided to wear jeans today?

"You're still thinking too loudly," she said. "Believe me when I say, I can come up with ways to make sure you stop."

The grip on my hair pulled my head back another inch. A high sound that I refused to describe as a whimper was born and died in the back of my throat. It... wasn't a protest, exactly. With a small jolt, I realized that for that moment in time, every single thought had fallen out of my head like Scrabble tiles dumped from the box. They lay in a jumble somewhere beneath me—unreadable nonsense waiting for someone else to pick them up and make sense of them.

Some of the long-held tension slid out of my spine.

"There now," Alex said, gentling her grip in favor of guiding me to rest my head on the edge of the couch cushion next to her thigh.

I breathed in her smell—clean sandalwood and the complex sweetness of night jasmine. Her fingers that had been harsh and unyielding before grew soft, stroking through my hair and making me shiver. A wavering sigh emptied my lungs, and I tried to resist the sudden, irrational urge to weep.

Fucking heat pheromones. They weren't even *mine*.

"We can stay like this for a bit," she said. "There's nothing else you need to do except feel whatever you're feeling. Sometimes feeling shit like that sucks, but locking it away sucks worse in the long run. Ask me how I know." The last few words were an exhausted sigh.

I reached my hand out and covered her knee, my body moving before my mind could come up with a dozen reasons why it was a bad idea. Her fingers stilled in my hair for a moment, but then she resumed the soothing rhythm.

Time passed. Whenever my shoulders started to tense up, Alex's hand tightened in my hair, the shivery almost-pain abruptly clearing my thoughts again, and only relenting when I went limp and compliant in her grip.

It shouldn't have meant anything. It was… nothing, really. A fist in my hair, or a light stroking over my scalp. Punishment and reward. And yet, the minutes ticked by, becoming hours, and somehow I ended up lying on the couch instead of kneeling on the floor. More time passed, and I found my head pillowed on the alpha's thigh.

How had that happened?

Eventually, the achy oversensitivity in my cock eased as the air cleared a bit, Leo's pheromone production waning during the valley between heat peaks.

Even so, I was *aware* of my body in a way I usually tried to avoid—probably because there was nothing else for me to think about right now. Or at least, nothing that didn't immediately result in my hair getting pulled until I stopped.

My body was such an odd thing. I hated it, while knowing objectively that it wasn't fair of me to feel that way. It wasn't my body's fault that its insides had been raped and scarred by monsters who thought they owned me and could rip out whatever parts of me didn't meet with their approval. It wasn't my body's fault that I injected it with testosterone and worked it to exhaustion in the gym, so I would look more like a beta.

My physical form had always done its best for me. Hell, it had even saved my mating gland by being left-handed—hiding that part of me on my left shoulder rather than my right one, where the butchers had assumed it would be. That little gland was still gamely churning out weak omega perfume, despite everything it had endured and continued to endure.

For the first time in what felt like a very long time, I listened to my body instead of trying to tune it out. It was oddly peaceful; my physicality settling around me like a familiar cloak in this warm, soft room full of alphas who had promised to watch over us.

Was this strange interlude helping Alex find a sense of peace with her ghosts as well? It was clear she had quite a collection of things haunting her, even if I didn't know the details. I wasn't sure if it was helping her or not. She wasn't purring—but she was at least focused enough on me that she'd sensed every single time my mind started to wander back to my worries. Surely that couldn't leave room for much else, could it?

Right on cue, her hand tightened, sending shivery tingles from my scalp down the length of my spine. I released a breathless moan and went limp again, making a point of nuzzling into her thigh as she returned to stroking me.

At some point, relaxation morphed into dozing. I awoke to the feeling of slender fingers playing over my mating gland, raising gooseflesh across my chest and arms. Weak perfume or no, the gland was a fairly useless appendage at this point. Without enough omega hormones circulating to regulate it, there was no way it could perform its intended function of bonding me to one or more alphas. It was still sensitive, though—and Alex's light touch drew a low whine from my throat.

"I sure do like the sound of that," Flynn said.

"It did sound like a good noise," Jax agreed.

Flynn stretched in the nest, scenting the base of Leo's neck as he did. "She's waking up," he said. "She'll be ready for the next round pretty soon, I'll wager."

Leo stretched as well, unconsciously mirroring the alpha behind her. "M'awake," she murmured, sounding anything but. Her bleary hazel eyes ran around the room, falling on me in my alpha-drugged haze. She smiled, an expression like the sun coming out. As it always did, it made me want to kiss her or collapse into tears, or maybe both at the same time.

"*Odama*," she said softly.

I swallowed, my throat clicking.

Jax approached, giving Alex a questioning look that asked her permission before he settled down across from us.

"Hey, Kam. Are you ready to talk to us yet?" he asked.

I licked my lips. "I hate what was done to my body. I don't think I can enjoy sex. And part of me wants to know for sure, but I'm also afraid to find out." The words poured out like water from a broken jar.

Jax nodded. "You've tried before?"

Leo crawled over to me and climbed onto the couch, squeezing in behind me and laying her head on my hip. "With me," she said. "But not with alphas." Her honey and orange blossom scent wrapped around me, further sensitizing my skin.

"We used black market alpha pheromones," I said.

Flynn made a disgusted noise, joining the rest of us and flopping down next to Jax. "Coulda just asked and had the real thing, Ginger Tea."

Jax elbowed him, and Flynn responded with a warning growl.

Flynn gestured between himself, Jax, and Leo. "Did any of this do it for you? Get you going earlier?"

"Yes," I said, "but getting aroused and getting off are two different things."

It felt surprisingly cathartic to just blurt it all out; throw the ugly, bleeding stump of my omega reproductive system on the ground so the others could stare at it.

Flynn shrugged. "Yeah. Like I told you in Romania, I've been with a couple of sterilized omegas. One could still get off and the other couldn't." He tapped the side of his head. "I get the impression that a lot of it has to do with what's going on up here. And no offense, Ginger Tea, but your brain is one big tangle most of the time. This is only the second time I can think of when I've seen you let go."

I flushed, glad my olive complexion would hide the blood rushing to my cheeks. The other time had been when I'd lost my shit and sobbed in Flynn's arms after Beckett and his pack had rescued us in Romania and whisked us away to safety.

"Uhh," I said.

"Leo's gonna start climbing toward her next peak soon," Flynn said. "And the pheromones will be flying again. Jax'll take care of her this time. While he's doing that, I want to see if Alex and me can get you off between us. So, Alex? You up for that? Because you can't get him pregnant and you can't accidentally mate him, so your usual excuses won't cut it."

It was blunt to the point of cruelty—explicitly defining the things that made me feel broken—but the obvious lack of any intent to hurt allowed Flynn's words to slide off me without sticking. These were facts. Everyone here knew them. The truth of them existed whether anyone said them aloud or not.

I wasn't sure how Alex would respond, though. A touch on my chin turned my head until I was looking up at her.

"Is that what you want?" she asked, her green gaze holding mine.

I blinked. Was it what I wanted?

Leo poked me in the hip, and I flinched in surprise. "It's eating you up not knowing," she said.

I frowned at her. "Aren't you supposed to have heat-brain right now?"

She shrugged, unapologetic. "It feels different this time."

"She's not coming off blockers," Jax said. "This is a normal heat, not a crazy rebound heat spent imprisoned in a terrorist cell with an alpha she doesn't know."

"What he said," she agreed. "Now answer the question before my brain *does* get stupid again."

"Y-yes?" I said, sounding like the wishy-washiest omega on the planet.

"Cool," Flynn said. "Now take your damned clothes off. Why are there still so many fucking clothes on in this room?"

He was naked. So was Leo, though I wasn't entirely sure whether she was aware of the fact. The rest of us were still fully clothed—

Jax had even put a shirt back on after the first round.

There was something important left to address, though. I looked up at Alex again. "You haven't said yes."

The alpha seemed to shake herself free of some sort of reverie. "Told you earlier," she said. "We're here to give you both everything you need." There was a careful sort of distance in her expression, but no hesitation in her tone.

Flynn clapped his hands and rubbed them together. "Right. First, I want to see you and Leona together. I already know what you can do for her when she's horny and craving a knot, and it's hot as fuck. But I wanna see what she does for you, too."

I rolled onto my back to better see Leo. She crawled up my body and took my face between her hands. "I love you, Kameron Patel," she said. "You know that, right?"

I mirrored her, capturing her face in my palms. "Of course I do. I love you, too, *odama*."

She pressed forward and kissed me, like we'd kissed so many times before. For a moment, I could almost forget that my head was lying on an alpha's thigh and Leo was leaking slick onto my jeans. But I was still in that surreal place of being fully connected to my body, and she was pumping out heat pheromones with ever-increasing intensity. In no time, the tight, achy feeling began to slide over me again.

"You'll feel better with your clothes off," she murmured against my lips, as though she could read my mind. "Trust me on this one."

I sighed. "Right. Let me up, then."

Leona rolled off me, and I sat up, feeling hopelessly self-conscious and awkward as I reached for the buttons of my shirt. I tried to take in the others with glances quick enough not to count as real eye contact. Jax was frowning. So was Leo. Flynn looked thoughtful. Alex, by contrast, was drilling holes through me with her green eyes. I flushed again beneath the weight of that heavy alpha gaze, not liking this feeling of being hot and bothered while knowing it was likely to lead nowhere except frustration.

I hated the fact that I felt like this, having to make decisions about every little thing. Getting undressed… deciding what Leona and I should try to do together… deciding what I did or didn't want the alphas to do.

I *hated* it.

"Stop," Alex said, a full-on alpha bark.

My spine snapped straight, my hands freezing on my half-open shirt, even as a humiliating sense of relief swept through me.

"Yes, alpha," I breathed.

She stood up, straightening to her full height and looming over me. "This isn't what you want. Enough dissembling. Tell me—*right now*—exactly what you need."

The alpha power in her voice took the choice of whether or not to answer away from me. I was an omega, and broken or not, I *would* obey an alpha's command.

"I don't want to have to make these choices," I said with a gasp. "I want someone else to make them for me. I just want to be…"

I trailed off, thinking of Flynn's words. *It's our Ginger Tea here who wants to be pinned down by the throat and used over and over until he breaks.* A shiver trickled down my spine.

"*Used*," I finished miserably.

SIX

Kameron

"OH, *KAM*," Leo murmured. I wondered if she was thinking of how gently she'd always treated me when we were intimate, and a fresh surge of guilt hit me.

"Told ya," Flynn said under his breath.

Alex shot him a quelling look.

"You want it not to be about you at all," she offered, her voice losing its bark.

"Yes," I said, with utter relief at the understanding in her tone. My shoulders slumped, my chin dropping to rest on my chest. "Please, just... do it to me? Make me take it. I don't want to have responsibility for what happens to me."

Alex and Jax exchanged a long look, an entire wordless conversation taking place between them.

"He's perfuming, even if it's faint," Jax said. "If he's in genuine distress at any point, we'll be able to smell it."

Alex hesitated for only a moment. Then she gave a single nod.

I should have been irritated that they were discussing me in the third person. Instead, my anxiety faded, replaced by a shaky sense of calm because the alphas were taking control. My hands fell to lie limply in my lap, the buttons of my shirt forgotten.

"Leona." Jax's voice radiated alpha reassurance. "Give your *odama* a hug, and then let's give the others some space for a bit. Can you scent him?"

"Yes," Leo said, her hazel eyes very wide.

"Then we'll know if anything's upsetting him," he said firmly. "Otherwise, he needs his alphas right now, not us."

Leo chewed her lower lip for a moment before nodding reluctant agreement. She wavered to her feet, the next peak already coming up on her. When her arms came around me, I hugged her back tightly.

"They're going to take care of you," she murmured, and pressed her lips to my mating gland in a gentle kiss.

I couldn't speak, so I buried my face in her fiery hair for a moment before letting her go. Jax extended a hand to her, and after a final long glance at me, she took it.

"So, can I play with him now, Alex?" Flynn asked, once the pair had crossed to the far side of the nest and claimed a spot.

My heart beat faster. Prickly sweat broke out across my back.

"Go ahead," Alex said, taking a seat on the other side of the sectional and crossing one leg over the other like a queen on her throne. "Let's see what we've got to work with here."

"About damn time," Flynn said.

Before I could draw breath, he was in front of me—his big hands grasping the material of my shirt and yanking it open. Buttons popped loose as he manhandled me around and pulled the shirt down below my elbows. My cuffs were still fastened, the fabric trapping my arms behind me by the wrists. Flynn wrapped the material around and around, tangling me further, and my body went hot all over.

Trapped.

A high-pitched noise escaped my throat and I tried to squirm away, only to end up on my back on the couch barely a heartbeat later. I jerked my shoulders, attempting to free my arms to no avail.

"Nuh-uh," Flynn said. His hand closed loosely over my throat. "None of that now, little omega."

Pinned.

"Let me up," I whispered, desperate to make sure he was really in charge... that my choices really didn't matter to him.

"No," he said, his free hand tugging at the fastenings of my jeans. He pulled them down roughly, heedless of my half-hard and painfully oversensitive cock. His scent of musk and cardamom was nearly overpowering, twining with the other alphas' scents and Leo's heat perfume. From the other side of the nest, I could hear her breathy gasps as Jax did... *something*... to her.

My nipples hardened to aching points.

"Hmm. Seems like we should be able to do some good with this," Flynn mused, and closed a meaty hand around my shaft.

It was too much, *too much*. I keened, trying to scrabble backward on the sectional with my legs trapped by my jeans and my arms trapped by my shirt. The hand on my throat tightened in warning.

"*Stay*," Flynn ordered, like someone might command a dog.

I shuddered, compelled by the alpha's command… forced to lie there and feel what he was doing to my body, whether I wanted to or not. On the other side of the room, Leo whimpered and cried out, the unmistakable sound of an omega having an earth-shattering orgasm administered by an alpha. My body thrummed with overstimulation as Flynn's callused hand squeezed and kneaded my cock, forcing it momentarily to full hardness.

He paused long enough to spit on his palm before wrapping his hand around me again and pumping… not gently. I knew how this would go, even if I couldn't do anything about it under the circumstances. It would be overwhelming at first, before becoming tolerable and even pleasant for a time, after which it would grow uncomfortable, then painful, and eventually unbearably excruciating.

I lay tense beneath Flynn's grip, my pulse fluttering against his fingers on my throat. Liquid heat slowly began to build in my gut, distracting me from the overstimulation and eventually replacing it. A moan wrenched free of my lips, and as though that had been some kind of a signal, Flynn let go of my cock. It wilted almost immediately in the absence of direct stimulation, but the heavy, warm feeling in my stomach lingered.

"Think that's enough of that for a bit, huh, Ginger Tea?" he said, not waiting for a reply. "Let's see about those pretty brown tits of yours next. They're awfully hard, considering how warm it is in here."

He thumbed my left nipple. A sharp tingle zinged along my nerves. Gooseflesh erupted across my chest as I swallowed a gasp. His fingers closed over the pebbled point, pinching and tugging sharply. I arched off the couch cushion with a strangled yelp.

He chuckled. "Bet you felt that in all four of them, didn't ya?"

"They cut out two," I whispered, knowing he would be able to see the small, jagged scars.

Flynn grunted and pinched the other nipple. I jerked at the phantom sensation.

"Maybe. But if I can still make you feel 'em, are they really gone?" he asked.

I might have answered, except it was too hard to focus on words with Flynn torturing my chest, alternating pinches with scrapes of his blunt fingernails until I was a breathless, squirming mess.

"Well, that was fun," he said. "We'll have to do some more of that later."

I managed a strangled '*hngh*' noise, too wrecked to move even when the hand around my throat disappeared. A muffled, high-pitched cry came from Leo's corner, and I turned my blurry gaze to find her draped over Jax in a sixty-nine position with his head buried between her thighs and his giant cock down her throat. As though she sensed me looking, she opened her eyes and met mine with a look equally as glassy.

Flynn pulled my jeans down and off, leaving me naked except for the shirt still tangled around my arms. "You ready for him now, Alex?" he called.

"Bring him over," she said.

I blinked, having completely missed it whenever she'd risen from the couch and removed her clothing. She reclined in the dip of the ridiculous sex divan—upper body resting against the taller end that acted as a backrest; legs straddling the seat to expose the folds between her legs, feet braced flat on the floor.

God, she was... magnificent. The polar opposite of Leo's omega softness, with her small, vestigial breasts over ripped pecs, and a sinuous, lean-muscled body that belonged on ancient statuary somewhere.

Flynn—equally impressive, but in an entirely male and overpowering way—watched me ogling his pack alpha with an amused huff. "Come on, Ginger Tea. Time to make yourself useful."

He leaned down and hoisted me over his shoulder before I even knew what was happening, clamping a hand over my bare ass to steady me. Flynn rose as though I weighed nothing and carted me over to the sex couch. He deposited me on my knees at the foot of the thing—worshipping at Alex's altar, so to speak.

Flynn gestured at her. "Go on," he said. "Get her ready while I get you ready. Use your mouth, in case that's not obvious."

Since no one had bothered to untangle my arms from behind me, it was, in fact, pretty obvious. I blinked up at Alex, reclining in front of me.

"Come here, omega," she said.

There was no way to comply except to slither onto the end of the sex couch on my belly, and neither of the alphas seemed to care how awkward and ridiculous that looked.

Because this wasn't about me.

This was about an omega giving an alpha pleasure in the heat-nest. It didn't matter if my womb was gone and my passage was sewn shut, because my mouth still worked and that was what Alex wanted to use right now. The realization shook something loose inside me.

I managed to get my hips draped over the swell at the low end of the divan, but without the use of my arms, I was stymied when it came to getting my mouth where it needed to be. God, I could smell her—*right there*, but just out of reach. I'd never been this close to a female alpha's sex. I wanted to be even closer.

There was a mystique around female alphas, even among purebreds. Before things had gone to hell, I'd been just old enough to join the secretive cliques of prepubescent omegas who passed around naughty photos of naked female alphas, along with faded copies of diagrams from biology textbooks that had been banned decades earlier.

Hyenas, the betas called them, for the superficial resemblance to a species whose females had pseudo-phalluses visually indistinguishable from the males' penises. Female alphas' clits resided inside a sheath until they were stimulated, at which point they emerged as they grew erect. They were about the same length as a male beta's cock, but lacked the girth. If the schoolyard whispers were to be believed, the knots made up for it.

I had a pretty good idea where that knot was going to end up today, and the thought tightened something low in my gut. It might have been trepidation. It might have been something else.

Alex took pity on me and grasped my hair, dragging my head up until my mouth was where she wanted it. "Lick," she ordered.

I did, drowning in the scent of sweet sandalwood as Leo whimpered out another orgasm somewhere behind me. My cock throbbed, trapped against the buttery leather of the divan.

The tip of Alex's clit was already poking out from its hood. I traced the shape with my tongue, tasting salt and musk and the aromatic forests from around my native Kolkata. Had watching Flynn touch me excited her? Had she been watching Jax take Leo apart as well? The idea that we both might have had this effect on her sent a flutter of omega pride through my chest.

Behind me, the unmistakable sound of a plastic bottle cap being popped open made me freeze for a moment. Alex tugged on my hair, redirecting me to my purpose, and I gamely went back to licking and sucking her emerging length to hardness.

Cool liquid dribbled into the valley between my buttocks. I shivered and whined around my growing mouthful of alpha clit. Flynn, being Flynn, wasted no time in swirling a thick finger around the rim of my ass a couple of times and shoving it unceremoniously inside. I gasped at the burn and jerked my head back from Alex's sex.

She tightened her grip on my hair and put me right back where she wanted me, sucking on the slender, erect shaft that was already growing long enough to tickle the back of my throat as she thrust slowly in and out of my mouth.

Flynn's other hand landed on my left buttock with a sharp slap. I jerked and grunted, my ass clenching hard around his finger.

"Did anyone say you could stop, little omega?" he asked cheerfully. "Keep your mind on your job."

How I could be expected to keep my mind on anything under these circumstances was something of an open question—but of course, that was the entire point. The finger in my ass ached and burned unpleasantly, and *no one cared*. At least, not unless it genuinely hurt me to the point that it soured my scent.

The sounds and smells of sex were all around me. Normally, it would have been a reminder of what I couldn't have... of what I couldn't *provide*, as a ruined omega. But I was already a part of this. Alex was going to fuck me and knot me and come inside of me. She was fully hard in my mouth, even now.

Flynn was poking around in my ass like someone fumbling for a light switch in the dark, and I was still not *remotely* sold on gay betas' answer to penetrative sex. He hummed in consideration and pulled out, manhandling my hips higher and jamming one of the countless cushions beneath me to change the angle of my hips.

More lube, and two fingers pushed inside me. By rights, this should not have been an improvement—only, it kind of *was*. Alex pulled my mouth off her clit.

"Can't find it?" she asked cryptically.

"Gimme a minute," Flynn grumbled. "I think maybe it's... *ah*."

He twisted his fingers and stars exploded across my vision, stealing my breath.

"It's way up in there, all right," Flynn said, rubbing his fingertips over the same place again, with the same result. "Could be a pure-bred thing, I guess."

I writhed, unable to draw breath as he worked the magic spot with a steady rhythm. The sensation was difficult to describe — like I needed to come and piss and empty my bowels at the same time, despite the fact that I'd been perfectly fine a moment before. Mostly, though, I needed him *not to ever stop.*

"Oh, god," I choked out, my voice joining the chorus of Leo's moans.

"I think this'll work," Flynn was saying, addressing Alex as though I wasn't even present. "We'll just need to hit him with everything at once and not let up."

A third finger stretched my entrance, and although Flynn was no longer sliding his fingertips over that spot, my body still vibrated like a struck gong. I breathed rapidly through my nose, feeling as though I was losing control of my muscles and my thoughts in equal measure.

"Our girl over here is just about ready for another knot," Jax called. "Can we help at all?"

"Yeah, come on over and join the party," Flynn replied, twisting his wrist again and dragging a gasp from me. "Grab one of the small condoms for Alex while you're at it. It'll make cleanup easier."

I heard Jax murmur something sweet and encouraging to Leo, who moaned. A moment later, something shiny arced through the air and Alex caught it one-handed. I watched with parted lips as she tore the foil packet open and sheathed her slender shaft. She reached for the lube Flynn passed her and slicked up the condom before closing the cap and tossing the bottle aside.

"Get him up here," she said.

Flynn's thick fingers slid out of me, leaving me aching and empty. Before I had enough time to properly register the feeling, strong hands lifted and turned me to straddle Alex's lap, my back to her front. She gripped my hips, positioning me where she wanted me—and *dear god*, was she strong.

I only had a moment to think, *this is it, an alpha is going to take me*, when the tip of her hard clit nudged my entrance. My own body-weight pressed her inside, past the tight ring of my body's defenses. After Flynn's preparation, it should have been easy to take her—but she felt huge.

Overwhelmed, I tried to buck, to squirm away—but her hand tangled in the sweat-soaked shirt still binding my arms, and her knees hooked inside of mine spread me wide, splaying me open and helpless, with no leverage to lift myself.

"I've got you now, little omega," she said. The words sounded like a threat, but the tone was a promise.

My body clamored—for more, or for less—I wasn't sure. My breath came in shallow gulps. I tried to imagine what I must look like… hair disheveled, mouth swollen and red from the slide of Alex's shaft, legs forced wide, omega cock on display.

Trembling muscles gave up the fight one by one. Alex took my weight effortlessly, easing me back until I lay fully against her, my arms trapped against her six-pack abs, her small breasts pressing against my back. Her clit, buried deep inside me, brushed against that place Flynn had found earlier. A tremor rattled through my body, and I choked on air.

Jax deposited Leo in more or less the same position I'd been in before, except her arms weren't pinioned. I didn't know what my eyes looked like, but hers were dark and wanting, the pupils blown wide. With her hips supported on the curved end of the divan, she was basically presenting for the alpha behind her.

"Leo," I rasped, caught by how beautiful she looked like this—naked and debauched, ready to be filled by the blond god kneeling at her entrance. Jax slid into her, slow and deep, drawing a decadent moan from her bee-stung lips.

"Go on, sweet thing," Flynn rumbled. "Help us out, here. You know you want to taste him."

My heart kicked hard against my ribcage, but Leo's hands were already grabbing my thighs. Her skin was hot… feverish… but it was nothing to the heat of her mouth when her lips closed around my cock. I was hard, I realized. *Really* hard. Fully erect, and achingly sensitive.

The familiar feeling of *too much, too much* scorched its way up my spine. But again—no one here cared. They'd *promised* me they wouldn't care, wouldn't stop, wouldn't let me get away from them. I whimpered. Leona's fiery heat was somehow pouring out of her body and into mine. My nipples ached… all four of them… even though no one had touched them yet.

"Now there's a sight," Flynn said, standing next to the divan. "Guess I'll have his mouth, since everything else is already in use."

"Oh, fuck," I yelped, as Flynn fisted his cock with one hand and tangled his other hand in my hair, pulling me to him.

Alex rolled her hips, dragging the tip of her clit over the place inside me that sent stars across my vision. My mouth fell open, and Flynn pushed the head of his cock past my lips. I grunted a token protest, jerking against the restraint of my shirt, only to have my struggles ignored. Both Jax and Alex started moving, and the banked embers in my belly burst into flame.

Every deep thrust from Jax pushed Leo forward, shoving my cock down her throat. Every roll of Alex's hips set off fresh fireworks behind my watering eyes. Flynn's ridiculously huge cock stretched my lips wide. It was hard to breathe around him, which added to my growing lightheadedness and loss of control. My body was barreling toward a precipice that had nothing to do with my brain, and all I could do was come along for the ride.

A sharp tingling sensation began at the base of my spine, shivering along my nerves until my scalp started to prickle. Unfamiliar muscles within the cradle of my pelvis coiled, tensing. When I could get air at all, the smell of alpha and omega heat pheromones was choking—sweet and spicy, woodsy and pungent. My spine arched, my body going rigid as I tried to chase that elusive feeling coiling and writhing inside me.

Leo keened around my cock, reaching her peak as Jax pounded into her from behind. Her fingers curled convulsively around my thighs. I teetered on the edge of something, my body trying to follow her but not quite getting there as I struggled toward the apex.

Alex wrapped an arm around me, her fingers finding one of my remaining nipples and pinching hard. "Let go," she said simply.

The jolt of sensation from my nipple rocketed straight to my cock, and from there to the place where her clit was grinding inside me. Every muscle in my body locked solid, even as euphoria drenched me as though someone had poured it over my head from a bucket. I was seamlessly connected to all of the others caught in the throes of pleasure within the heat-nest, and for an endless moment, nothing else existed except that incomprehensible ecstasy.

My body jerked like a puppet on a string. Alex shuddered beneath me with a low groan. Her clit throbbed inside of me, and a new pressure grew as her knot swelled. Flynn slid out of my mouth, thumbing the trail of saliva from my lower lip with a gentle caress.

"Knew you could do it, Ginger Tea," he said, sounding pleased.

I huffed out a breath that was half a laugh and half a sob as my muscles went lax, a sense of indescribable well-being washing over me. Leo released my softening cock in favor of pressing messy, uncoordinated kisses on my inner thighs.

For some reason, tears were streaming down my cheeks in rivulets. I let Alex take my weight, my body stretching around the place where she was knotting me. She was so tall that the back of my head slotted neatly against the crook of her neck when I leaned against her. Her hand, still wrapped around me, settled over my heart.

"Rest now," she said, like it was an order.

I turned my tear-stained face toward her, letting her tuck my head beneath her chin, and did as my alpha told me.

SEVEN

Alex

I'D FORGOTTEN, damn it. I'd forgotten what it was like to be knot-deep in an omega, holding them as they came down from a crashing peak. Not that Irina had been carrying anything like the kind of baggage that Kameron Patel was carting around—but the emotions of the heat-nest were still the same.

It wasn't remotely like knotting an obliging beta male. I was drunk on Leona's heat pheromones, my own alpha hormones sloshing around my brain in a heady cocktail of *protect* and *mark* and *dominate* as Kameron's body fluttered and clenched around the swollen base of my clit. My mouth watered with the need to bite, for Christ's sake—and only the knowledge that doing so wouldn't accidentally initiate a bond kept me from freaking the fuck out.

Was I broken? Defective somehow? Did all of the self-control I exercised in *every other aspect of my life* mean nothing the moment I was around an omega in heat?

I'd been watching the others like a hawk, and there'd been no indication so far that biting had even entered their minds. *I've never been tempted to bite*, Jax had said, and maybe he'd been telling the truth. Maybe it was just me.

I swallowed saliva, smelling the faint hint of ginger and lemon through the heavier miasma of sweetness. The omega in my lap made a humming noise and nuzzled against my throat. His cheeks were wet. Something clenched painfully in my chest.

Flynn crouched beside the divan where the rest of us were piled in a messy tangle. He reached out one big hand and ran it through Leona's sweat-soaked hair. Her head was still resting on Kameron's thigh. Her body, limp as a dishrag, was draped over the lower end of the couch. Jax knelt behind her, apparently intending to let her ride out his knot right where she was. He murmured soothing nonsense to her, stroking his fingers up and down her spine. His focus was on her, just as it should be.

Flynn's focus, on the other hand, was on me. He gestured in a clear request for permission to touch Kameron while I was knotting him. I gave him a weary nod, stomping down on the ridiculous warning growl that wanted to rumble up from my chest.

My packmate laid his palm flat over Kameron's belly, fingers spread. The omega's breath puffed out in a sigh against the side of my neck.

"Did that feel good, Kam?" Flynn asked. "Did you like it when we made you come?"

Kameron nodded, not lifting his head from the crook of my neck. "Mm-hmm. 'S good. Thank you, alphas."

Flynn nodded as well. "You want it again, you just ask. We'll pin you down and make you come whenever you want. Lots of time to make up for, right?"

I tried not to tense up, not wanting to upset the omega still trapped on my knot. That hadn't sounded like Flynn was only talking about the period of the heat contract. In lieu of saying anything aloud, I directed a glare in his direction.

It bounced right off him.

"What about you, *alef*?" he asked me. "You doin' okay?"

And how the *hell* was I supposed to answer that?

"Fine," I managed.

And now Jax was shooting me worried glances as well. *Brilliant.*

"*Fine,*" I repeated more forcefully. Kameron let out a happy little gasp in response to the hint of a bark in my tone. He rolled his head to the side to bare his throat to me, which was *not* helping the situation, damn it. Leona didn't react at all—already down for the count, it seemed. The others had the good sense to back off.

I shoved everything out of my head as best I could, letting myself sink into the raw physicality of the joining instead, as I waited for my knot to go down.

———◆———

Later, as Leona dozed under Jax and Flynn's watchful gazes, I sat once more on the end of the sectional. I'd snatched a quick shower and put some clothes on. So had Kameron. He sat on the cushion-covered floor at my feet, with his back propped against the front of the couch, loosely hugging his knees.

The unrelenting aura of tension that usually hung over his head like a cloud was gone — it was amazing what a good fuck could do. Now, he merely appeared thoughtful.

"You're still thinking too loudly," I told him, somewhat against my better judgment.

He glanced up at me, surprised. "Really? I thought I was being admirably quiet about it this time."

I raised an eyebrow, and he huffed. "All right. Yes. I'm trying to decide if it's appropriate to ask a personal question. I've been leaning toward *no*."

I had a pretty good idea of what that question would be. "No, go ahead. You've had my clit up your ass. You might as well ask."

Honestly, I was kind of surprised Leona hadn't given him the complete rundown on my messy past already.

"Irina," he said quietly. "Who was she?"

I waited for the familiar tide of old pain to rise, crest, and slowly ebb. "Irina Pasternak was the omega I couldn't save. She was carrying our pups… and also my mating bite."

"Ah," Kameron said. Nothing else—no hollow sympathy, no request for further details.

"What about you?" I asked. I told myself it was just a way to redirect the conversation away from me, but the truth was, I was curious. These two must have had the devil's own luck to get as far as they had.

His shoulders rose and fell on a silent sigh. "I was born in Kolkata. The locals got tired of our purebred family being too prosperous and too comfortable with our own position. Committee sympathizers came for us when I was twelve, and I was the only one considered economically valuable enough to keep for the breeding pens. When I turned out not to be pliable enough for their tastes, they sterilized me and threw me into the slave market."

I waited while he gazed off into the distance. He'd summarized his past in a bland monologue, much as I had. I understood the need to tamp those emotions down. He turned and glanced at me before continuing in a more normal tone.

"The person who bought me was secretly working with the underground. She shipped me off to North America and arranged a beta identity for me."

"Lucky," I said.

"Yes, I suppose so," he agreed.

An oddly comfortable silence fell between us. I was aware of Jax and Flynn listening in on the conversation from across the room, but they didn't try to interrupt.

Kameron's story wasn't miles different from Irina's—though I wasn't about to say so aloud, given how hers had ended. Irina had at least escaped sterilization, but she, too, had been purchased by one of the underground operatives we called the *catch-and-releasers*. It had always enraged me that the best we could seem to come up with was this patchwork method of freeing individual alphas and omegas from slavery. What I really wanted was to put a torch to the entire damned institution and burn it to the ground.

This, clearly, was one of several reasons I was only a lowly foot soldier in the resistance, rather than a four-star general.

"Would you do something for me, please?" Kameron asked, some minutes later.

Tension coiled in my shoulders, but I'd been the one to insist that any omega in my pack's nest would get exactly what they needed, no matter what that was.

"Yes?" I said.

He released his grip around his knees, his posture going loose-limbed and exhausted. "As, er, *enlightening* as the experience was, I don't think I'm going to be in any kind of shape to play host to a knot for the next day or two."

Flynn snorted, but—somewhat surprisingly—kept any off-color commentary about female alpha knots to himself.

Kameron wisely ignored him. "That being said, I am so tired right now I can barely see straight. I, uh... I haven't been sleeping well lately."

That was obvious enough from the dark bags under his eyes. "Tell me what you need," I said.

He hesitated. "Would you watch over things while I rest? I mean—I know you were doing that already," he hurried to add. "What I'm asking is..." He trailed off.

"He wants you to watch over *him*," Flynn said. "Ginger Tea, no offense, but you're still really bad at asking for things."

Kameron ducked his head, not denying the allegation. An unpleasant mix of dread and longing tugged at me, but there was no avoiding the promise I'd made to look after his needs. I scooted forward, lowering myself off the couch and into the nest—trying not to feel awkward about it.

"Come on, then," I said, cringing inwardly at how painfully useless I was at things like this.

Flynn rolled his eyes at me. Jax lifted an eyebrow. "Will wonders never cease," he muttered. I mentally planned the kind of sparring sessions for them that would leave both of them bruised and aching for a week.

Kameron, blushing hard enough that it was visible even with his rich olive skin tone, curled up next to me in the soft nest and rested his head on my thigh. My hand lifted to stroke through his thick, silky hair, seemingly of its own volition. He drew in a slow, careful breath, and when he let it out, I felt his muscles grow slack with relief.

"Thank you alpha," he murmured.

I didn't reply — but I did keep stroking his hair... while trying my best to ignore the knowing looks that my packmates were giving me.

⬥

Jax and Flynn took turns knotting Leona through the rest of her heat. I maintained a martial eye on the birth control situation, ensuring that her cervical cap was removed and replaced at the appropriate intervals.

No one could have slept through her increasingly wild peaks, but Kameron still slept *a lot*. He probably needed it, especially since Flynn talked him into a second round of sex after he'd had a couple of days to recover from the first one. Well, I say *talked*. The others had grown increasingly feral and growly as the heat progressed, so it was more a case of Flynn having pinned Kameron on his back and straddled his hips to keep him there, before informing the omega that he was going to come this time with my clit up his ass and

Leona sitting on his face, drowning him in slick.

As I thrust into his pliant body some time later, angling my hips to give Jax room to administer a fiendishly thorough handjob at the same time, it occurred to me that I might have seriously underestimated the depths of my packmates' sexual depravity. That was right before Leona—straddling Kameron's face as promised—keened out an orgasm, her huge hazel eyes going distant and hazy. The fresh flood of pheromones triggered Kam, and his thrashing and clenching triggered me. I was only distantly aware of the snarls and moans as Flynn dragged Leona off of Kameron's face, fucking into her from behind while Jax knelt in front of her and fed her his cock.

Eventually, inevitably, Leona's heat subsided. I let the others pamper the two omegas with baths and blankets and an endless supply of food. At one point, Kameron flopped down next to me on the sectional and handed me a plate with a sandwich on it.

"Well," he said. "That was certainly..." He trailed off, looking more than a little dazed.

"Yeah," I agreed, and bit into the sandwich.

Though clearly exhausted, Leona McCready was *glowing*. There really wasn't another word for it. We both watched her with something like fascination.

Kameron sighed. "So, is it too soon to start talking about what comes next?"

I shrugged. "I'd be more than happy to, except I won't know the answer to that question until Beckett gets back from his meetings with the higher-ups. He should be here tomorrow."

But *tomorrow* came and went with no sign of the man. So did the following day. The morning after that, there was no denying the obvious conclusion. Something had happened to our team leader, and the five of us were potentially screwed beyond belief.

EIGHT

Leona

I WAS GOING to be sore for days, and I couldn't even be mad about it. My heat spent with Kam and our three alphas had been blissful, right up until the horrors of the outside world intruded on our cozy nest—as had always been inevitable.

The morning after I managed to recover from my heat-high and subsequent crash, Flynn had looked at me over breakfast and said, "You know it could be like this all the time, sweet thing. All you and your *odama* need to do is say yes."

And I'd wanted it. Oh, how I'd wanted it. In fact, I'd wanted it badly enough that instead of saying no like a rational person, I'd met Kam's eyes for a moment's silent conversation before turning back to Flynn and replying, "Ask us again after we've made things better in the world."

Then, as if I'd singlehandedly manifested disaster by daring to dream of a better future, Beckett failed to return. Two days passed beyond the deadline when he should have been back, and the alphas were in crisis mode.

Meanwhile, Kam and I were in the maddening position of being worse than useless. Not only were we no help when it came to tracking Beckett down, but our status as fugitive omegas meant we needed protecting.

At the sound of a vehicle crunching up the winding gravel drive, Jax and Flynn were up and heading for the front door in near-unison. Alex had gone to check in with a contact—a man Beckett supposedly would have left a message with, if he'd been unavoidably detained but was otherwise okay.

The familiar white Jeep pulled up and parked. Alex slid out and slammed the driver's door behind her, looking focused and deadly as she marched up to the house. Jax let her in.

"Well?" he asked.

"Nothing," she bit out. "Beckett didn't contact the guy. So the next step is to decide if we're going to bug out and try to join some other cell in the underground, or follow Beckett's tracks and try to figure out what happened to him."

"We go after Beckett," Flynn said without hesitation. "Obviously."

"It's not that simple," Alex shot back. "Not now."

"Because of us," I hazarded, gesturing between Kam and me. "Don't let us get in your way. We can fend for ourselves if we have to."

It wasn't a lie, although there was no question we'd be a lot more vulnerable without this pack of alphas protecting us. I'd been dragged from my apartment at three a.m. with nothing but the flimsy nightgown I'd been wearing, but Kam had ten thousand dollars in cash, along with a few personal belongings. That money would help pay for my escape as well as his— even if the idea of fleeing the country and leaving the others behind made me queasy.

But Alex shook her head. "It's partly that, yes; but there's also another consideration."

The muscles in Jax's square jaw twitched. "You need to leave me behind, too. I'm still not in fighting shape. I'd only slow you down."

I covered a wince. Though he was much better now, Jax was still recovering from muscle weakness and nerve damage on his left side. I still seethed thinking of those bastards in Romania who'd held us prisoner, injecting Jax with their poisonous experimental weapon designed to kill alphas and omegas while leaving betas unharmed.

Kam cleared his throat. My packmate had been uncharacteristically subdued since my heat ended—still processing things, I suspected. Now, though, he spoke up.

"Then Jax should stay here and guard us while Flynn goes with you, Alex," he said. "It's the most logical use of resources. From what I gather, it would be dangerous for Beckett to end up in the Committee's hands. He knows too much."

Flynn tapped his fingers against the wall. "He's right. There's the identity of Beckett's mate to worry about, for one thing."

Beckett was the only mated omega I'd ever met. The secrecy surrounding the identity of his partner was absolute, and the others had speculated that he or she must be someone high up in the organizational structure of the underground. If whoever had captured Beckett managed to pry that information out of him, it could potentially cause untold damage to the alphomic resistance.

"Is there any reason to think the location of this place has been compromised?" I asked.

"That depends entirely on who has Beckett right now, and how good they are at torturing people for information," Alex said tightly.

A chill skittered down my spine, but I squared my shoulders. "Any *concrete* reason?" I pressed.

"No," she admitted, before adding, "There's also no concrete reason to think it hasn't been compromised."

"I'm willing to take the risk," Kam said quietly. "Jax?"

Jax's tense posture said he wasn't happy at being left behind while his pack went into danger. Nevertheless, he gave a single, terse nod. "It makes sense. We'll need a second vehicle, though, in case we need to make a run for it. This place is in the middle of fucking nowhere."

"I think that's kind of the point," Flynn said. "Still, he's right."

Kam exchanged a glance with me. "We have ten thousand in cash. You should be able to pick up something cheap with a salvage title, and not have to dig too far into that amount."

"That'll work," Flynn said. "There ought to be some counterfeit or expired license plates hidden somewhere in this place. That's pretty standard for this kind of safehouse."

"What about you two?" I asked. "Do you have access to enough money for what you need to do? Gasoline, food, that kind of stuff?"

If they didn't, Kam and I would have to decide how much of our limited funds we were willing to throw at this mission. Ten thousand dollars was enough to smuggle two people out of the country, but it wasn't an extravagant amount. We could only afford to lose so much of it before one or both of us would be stuck here. And as omega fugitives, it wasn't as though we could easily get more money. We owed Beckett, though—we'd probably both be in the Committee's hands right now if not for his intervention.

"Let us worry about that," Alex said.

I had no idea if she meant they already had access to money, or if she planned to rob a bank, or what. But I was in no position to question the alphas—not when they had their shit together, and I totally didn't. I was still trapped in a strange limbo. My past life had been ripped away irretrievably, and I didn't know yet what the future would look like.

For a while, it had seemed like our future would be in the underground. With Beckett gone, that option might be lost to us. The uncertainty ate at me, now that the mindlessness of my heat had loosened its grip.

"Is this the plan we're going with?" Jax asked.

Alex hesitated before offering a sharp, affirmative nod. "It is. We'll acquire a second car before we leave. Flynn and I will track down the people Beckett went to meet with. We can at least find out if he made it to those meetings or not. We'll be back in four days. If we're delayed, or if we find a lead worth following, we'll leave a message with Beckett's contact— the one I spoke to today. If you have to leave this place before we get back, you do the same."

It concerned me that this was essentially an identical plan to the one Beckett had used, and that hadn't worked out very well for him. Unfortunately, I didn't have anything better to offer as an alternative.

"Right," Flynn said. "It's no good standing around here with our thumbs up our asses, in that case. Let's get moving."

<hr>

It took the rest of the day and half of the following one to get everything set up. Kam and I mostly stayed out of the way. With my photograph plastered all over the newspapers, it wasn't as though I could run to the nearest grocery store to pick up supplies.

In a role reversal from the past several days, Kam and I committed to ensuring that the others were fed and actually got some sleep. Flynn and Jax in particular were still recovering from four solid days of mating and guarding the nest during my heat. Alphas were tough, but that kind of thing took a toll. I figured the least we could do was pamper them a little.

Flynn acquired a sketchy looking Chrysler LeBaron, its hood and left front fender an entirely different color from the rest of the car.

"Frame's a bit twisted," he said. "It pulls to the right a little at highway speeds."

"So do I these days," Jax grumbled, accepting the keys.

Kam had unearthed the promised collection of license plates from a closet upstairs. He went outside to mount them on the Franken-Chrysler, lending the car a tissue-thin facade of legality.

With fresh supplies laid in and the transportation issue solved, Alex and Flynn wasted no time in packing their clothing and weapons—eager to depart before the trail grew any colder than it already was.

I stood in the entryway of the house, my arms crossed tightly, trying not to succumb to the sense of impending doom that threatened to swallow me whole. For a few short days, everything had been perfect. I'd known going in that it wasn't the kind of perfection that could last—not for people like us. And I'd *still* been suckered in.

A new purpose in life.

A pack of misfit alphas devoted to my pleasure, and to Kam's.

It was too perfect—not the way real life worked.

"C'mere," Flynn said, and reeled me in. He had his travel bag slung over one broad shoulder. I let myself be reeled, desperate for a final taste of his overpowering *alphaness*. He held me against his hard-muscled chest and kissed the top of my head.

"Be nice to Jax while we're gone," he rumbled against my temple. "He's gonna be climbing the walls. Guess you probably will be, too."

"Probably," I agreed.

"You know, fucking is really good for stress relief," he said conversationally. "Just throwing that out there."

I felt a flush rise to my cheeks—a ridiculous reaction, given the events of the past week.

"For god's *sake*, Flynn," Alex said, saving me the necessity of a reply.

Flynn shrugged, and let me go when I regained enough self-control to pull away. He reached for Kam next, taking him by the chin and rubbing a thumb possessively across his full lower lip. Kam drew in a sharp little breath.

"Be good until we get back, Ginger Tea," Flynn said. "Or don't—it's usually more fun that way. See you in a few days."

"Stay out of trouble, asshole," Jax said. "Good hunting, Alex."

Alex gave him a short nod, clearly not one for lengthy goodbyes. Her catlike green eyes played over us, her gaze catching momentarily on Kam before she jerked it away.

"*Au revoir*," she said, and led Flynn out the front door.

We watched as the pair climbed into the Jeep. The engine turned over, and the vehicle headed away, leaving the Chrysler sitting alone and looking vaguely forlorn in the overgrown circle drive.

NINE

Leona

JAX SPENT the first day after Flynn and Alex departed stringing booby traps across all of the trails and tracks leading to the house. Fishing line—attached to every can, jug, and piece of metal trash we could find—now crisscrossed any trail large enough to accommodate people, strung inconspicuously at ankle height. Any intruder would trip the line and set off a cacophony of noise from the items secreted in the underbrush.

Despite the brisk nights, windows stood open on all sides of the house, letting in the sounds from outside so sensitive alpha and omega hearing could more easily pick up the noise of a trap being sprung. Jax set up a rotation schedule for guarding the house—eight hours on and sixteen hours off for each of us, during which we kept constant watch on the driveway and listened for disturbances coming from any other direction.

Jax was, of course, armed. But neither Kam nor I had any familiarity with firearms, and the noise involved in trying to learn on the fly would have drawn too much attention to our secret hideout. So as far as I could tell, our grand strategic plan in case of emergency was to run and get the alpha so he could shoot at whoever was trying to capture us. As battle strategy went, it didn't sound all that promising.

In fact, the current situation was eerily reminiscent of the way Kam and I had lived for years. We'd thrown together an iffy escape plan for when the worst inevitably happened, then sat back and waited for things to implode—because there was really no other option.

This felt very much like that, only dialed up to eleven.

As unregistered omegas, Kam and I had largely managed to ignore the potential for disaster as we lived our day-to-day lives. We'd have gone crazy otherwise. Maybe it was the difference in alpha versus omega psychology, because by contrast, Jax seemed hyper-focused on the danger twenty-four hours a day. I appreciated his dedication, but it was also exhausting.

With our assigned eight-hour shifts, it meant whichever two of us weren't watching for danger were pretty much left to our own devices the rest of the time. It didn't take long for me to start pondering Flynn's parting words to me.

You know, fucking is really good for stress relief. Just throwing that out there.

Jax had taken the three a.m. to eleven a.m. shift, since that was the roughest one. Kam had claimed seven p.m. to three a.m. since he was prone to insomnia anyway, leaving me with the cushy eleven-to-seven daytime shift.

When Kam showed up on the second evening to relieve me, he wrapped me up in his arms and pressed a kiss to my temple before pulling back to meet my eyes.

"How do you feel about using omega wiles to manipulate a stubborn alpha?" he asked.

I blinked at him. "I think I'm fresh out of wiles," I said uncertainly.

"Uh, no. Trust me, you're *really* not," he shot back. "Would you please do me a favor and turn Jax's brain off for a few hours before his skull bursts into flame or something? He's lovely, and I'm glad he's here, but he's also slowly driving me mad."

"I think he's just stressing out over the fact that he couldn't go after Beckett with the others," I said. "That's got to be rough on him. He's overcompensating, trying to keep us safe."

Kam patted my arm. "Yes. Which is why I'm siccing you on him. You have compassion for his situation. Whereas I mostly want to throw something at his head, and tell him that cleaning the same guns over and over won't magically make them more effective if someone sends a SWAT team after us."

I let out a startled laugh, even though nothing about it was remotely funny.

"Right," I told him. "Fair enough—I'm on it. But just so you know, you're starting to think like Flynn. I want you to really stop and ponder that while you're busy staring fixedly at an empty driveway for the next eight hours."

He patted my arm again and took up my post. "I love you, but I also reject your hypothesis in the strongest possible terms, *odama*. Go be wily, and I'll come find you in the nest when I get off-shift later. There's food in the fridge if you're hungry."

"Thanks," I said, and then added, "I think."

I left him to it. After a meal of cold leftovers, I headed upstairs and tracked down our wayward alpha in one of the spare bedrooms. Kam had been one hundred percent serious— Jax was seated at an old desk with one gun in his shoulder holster and the other in pieces in front of him, polishing one of the disassembled bits with a black-smudged rag.

"Hi," I said. "Rammed any good holes lately?"

He did a comical double take in my direction. I smiled sweetly and indicated the pistol on the desk. Understanding dawned, and he did at least have the good grace to look sheepish.

"It helps me relax," he explained.

I raised an eyebrow. "Good god—in that case, I'd hate to see you when you *haven't* been obsessively cleaning and oiling your guns."

He set the oddly shaped piece of metal aside. "Kam sent you, I take it?"

I nodded. "Mm-hmm. You're slowly driving him insane with your hyper-preparedness, apparently."

"Ah," he said. "Sorry."

I shrugged. "Don't take it personally. I think it's just that we're used to trying our best to ignore the guillotine hanging over our heads when it's not actively falling on us. Less stressful that way."

He shot me a wry look. "Maybe for you."

"Tell you what," I offered. "Let's keep each other company instead. Put that thing back together while I go take care of something. Back in a bit." I felt his eyes on me as I left the room and went down the hall to the nest, and the bathroom beyond it.

Something had changed in me over the past couple of weeks—besides the inevitable change that comes from having your life upended and the resulting debris set on fire. Or maybe that was part of it, too; it was hard to tell. Whatever the case, my usual sense of living on borrowed time had shifted in some indefinable way. I'd come to realize that, in many ways, I *hadn't* been living before. Not really. I'd only been existing, which was a very different thing.

I let myself into the extravagant bathroom and crossed to the sunken tub, where I crouched to plug the drain and turn on the tap. While it was filling, I stripped off and took a very quick shower in the separate stall, shampooing my mass of red hair and massaging conditioner into it. When I was done, I toweled off, leaving it hanging down in wet ringlets.

With a towel wrapped around my naked body, I adjusted the temperature of the bath a bit warmer and let it finish filling before turning off the taps. Then, I went to employ wiles against an alpha for probably the first time in my life.

———————◆———————

Jax's piercing blue eyes darkened as he took me in, a hint of the feral alpha who'd knotted me so possessively during my heat peeking through the veneer of an otherwise thoroughly civilized man. I stood dripping on the threshold, my chin tilted to show him a hint of throat as I looked at him through heavy lashes.

"Come with me, alpha," I said without artifice. "We need to relax for an hour or so, and then we need to sleep."

I saw him wrest back control of his libido; saw the regret coloring his gaze.

"I need to be ready in case anything happens," he said. "I'm sorry, Leona."

But I wasn't having it. "Does being naked and wet make your aim with those things worse?" I asked, indicating the pair of guns.

He frowned. "That's not—"

"Will being fully clothed make the odds any better if a Committee SWAT team shows up to surround the house?" I pressed.

He let out a sigh. "Probably not, but waving my dick at them as I'm hauled off wouldn't be a very dignified way to go out."

"Neither was being dragged out of bed in the middle of the night wearing a silk nightgown and no underwear," I said dryly. "And yet, here we both are."

I saw reluctant agreement soften the line of his shoulders.

"You want me to come take a bath with you?" he said, as though trying the words on for size.

I nodded. "Kam said I should use my omega wiles to get you to unwind for a bit before you drive him completely around the bend." I batted my eyelashes at him ridiculously. "Is it working?"

He laughed despite himself. "So, this must be how you negotiate international treaties, huh?"

I glanced down at my towel. "Well, I mean, I usually negotiated while wearing a few more clothes than this."

"Then you missed a trick. They wouldn't have known what hit them." He hauled himself to his feet and scooped up the now-reassembled gun. "Come on then, you wily little omega. But if I end up naked during a shootout, I reserve the right to say I told you so."

I smiled at him, unrepentant, and hoped desperately that things wouldn't come to that—because I would, in fact, feel pretty damned guilty if they did.

His slight limp was noticeable as he followed me back to the bathroom. I wondered if he would ever recover fully... and there was yet another thing for the guilt pile. That pile was in danger of growing out of control. However, it was also part of the past, not the present. None of it could be changed now.

I let my towel slip to the floor as I stepped through the doorway, not looking back at him as I crossed the bathroom and climbed onto the platform housing the huge sunken tub. Jax's gaze burned the back of my neck as I carefully stepped into the hot water and lowered myself down to lean against the edge with a happy sigh.

It was odd—I'd spent more time naked in the presence of other people in the last month than I had in the previous fifteen years combined. As an aligned omega with beta bloodlines, my body could pass a certain amount of scrutiny. But unregistered omegas did *not* seek out beta doctors, or otherwise put themselves in a position to be seen naked, if it was at all avoidable.

In the last few weeks, though, I'd been naked with Kam. I'd been naked with Jax, and with Flynn, and even with Alex—though I was pretty sure Alex would have run for the hills if she hadn't felt obligated to watch over her pack during the heat.

And I'd *liked* it.

I'd liked being seen. I'd liked being appreciated for my physical form. It was probably shallow of me... or maybe not. In a world that hated me because I was an omega, perhaps it was natural to crave that kind of acceptance from people who thought my hidden nature made me beautiful, rather than a freak.

Jax limped over to the tub and looked down at me, sending a frisson across my exposed skin.

"You really are stunning, Leona McCready," he said. "I hope you realize that."

I couldn't help the shy smile that tugged at my lips. "Well, you know, you're not so bad yourself." I raised my eyebrows. "From what I remember, at least. Maybe you'd better give me another look, just to be sure, though."

He snorted. "I'm a scarred reject from the breeding pens."

"You're a blond-haired, blue-eyed alpha Viking with bone structure that could cut glass," I corrected. "Not to mention, one of only three people I trust to protect my *odama* and my nest."

Jax exhaled a breath like it had been startled out of him. "Good god, woman—stop talking like that."

It did the trick, though. He started pulling off clothing, after setting the pair of holstered guns within easy reach. I ached in sympathy at the way he favored his left side, shrugging his shirt awkwardly over that shoulder.

And yet, it could have been so much worse. It still might be, once the Beta Liberation Front perfected their nerve agent into a targeted alphomic weapon. But they hadn't succeeded yet. I had to focus on that. They'd used Jax as a lab rat, but he was still alive. He hadn't died.

"Come here," I said, extending my hand to the scarred classical statue standing over me.

He gave me a long look and took it, allowing me to steady him as he lowered himself to sit on the edge of the tub. He paused a moment, then eased into the water with a long sigh.

"Good?" I asked.

"Yeah," he agreed.

I waited until he was settled before sliding across to straddle his lap. He was half-hard under the water. I leaned against him, and his arms immediately came around me as I buried my nose in the crook of his neck and breathed in his clean forest scent.

My heat cycle was well and truly over, but alpha arousal pheromones were still an aphrodisiac for omegas. My body grew warm and heavy against his. I could happily have sunk down on his cock and ridden him into mutual oblivion, now that I was no longer fertile and pregnancy wasn't a concern.

He made a noise of regret. "You're getting ideas. And while I like those ideas a lot, I'm gonna have to draw the line at knotting you when I'm supposed to be guarding you."

"I know," I said, not moving from my comfortable sprawl. "Tell me something, though. I understand that it's unpleasant popping a knot outside of actually mating. But I sucked you while Flynn was knotting me, and vice versa. Isn't that frustrating? Having sex but not coming?"

File this under *'things I never thought I'd be having a conversation about, especially while naked.'* But it wasn't awkward—not with Jax. It probably wouldn't have been with Flynn, either... though I was fairly sure trying to have this conversation with him would devolve into actual sex in an astonishingly short period of time.

"Not always," Jax said. "In the heat-nest, it's just a normal part of foreplay. We were taking turns with you, so it was a warm-up for the next round, if that makes sense."

"It does," I assured him.

"And it can be nice to get teased for a bit without it necessarily going further," he went on. "It kind of depends on the mood. There's nothing wrong with fooling around for fooling around's sake."

I pulled away enough to smile up at him. "Is that so?"

He stroked my wet hair back, giving me a wry look. "Why do I feel like you're asking me leading questions?"

Reaching a hand between our bodies, I wrapped my fingers around his heavy girth and gave him an experimental stroke. "Damn," I said. "There goes my clever subterfuge."

His summer-sky gaze went heavy lidded. A moment later, I was on my back in the tub with six-foot-plus of horny alpha on top of me, and no real awareness of how I'd gotten there. Warm water sloshed around my chin. I gasped, straining up, and was met by a pair of faintly chapped lips covering mine in a kiss that quickly turned filthy.

By the time he let me up for air, I was breathless.

The smell of cypress and musk filled my senses. One large hand rested between my shoulder blades, preventing me from sliding underwater. His touch guided me to arch my spine until the tips of my breasts broke the surface. His teeth closed around my right nipple, drawing an undignified whine from my throat. A pulse of hot slick turned my inner thighs slippery beneath the water.

It was possible I hadn't thought this plan all the way through.

"I miss your perfume," Jax said, and bit the other nipple.

I yelped, arching helplessly into the stimulation. "C-couldn't risk it in case we need to run," I managed.

He licked over the abused flesh, drawing a shudder and a fresh pulse of slick. "I know."

Twisting in the tub, he rearranged us so that he was sitting with his back propped against the side, and I was once more straddling him—facing away this time. His hand cupped my chin, drawing me back to rest against his chest with my throat bared and his hard cock nestled between my ass cheeks. His right hand moved confidently downward to cup my pussy, where I was slippery with arousal despite the water.

"I'm going to make you come," he said. "Twice. And then we're going to dry off and go into the nest, where I'm going to lay you out on a pile of pillows and fuck those beautiful breasts for a bit. When Kam comes back after his watch, he's going to find you naked and wrecked."

"Okay," I agreed breathlessly, my throat working against his light grip.

"Mmm," he said, and tipped my head, exposing the side of my neck opposite from my mating gland. I moaned as he kissed his way along it, and gasped when his teeth closed on the juncture of my neck and shoulder.

Something dark and primal rose within me, even though he was only playacting at a mating bite. Nevertheless, my body *knew*. His fingers slid the final inch, parting my folds, and we were off to the races.

TEN

Flynn

"SO, ARE WE gonna talk about this at some point, or what?" I asked, not taking my eyes off the highway unspooling beneath the Jeep's tires. Beside me in the passenger seat, Alex shifted restlessly.

"There's nothing to talk about," she said.

"Bullshit." I shot her a sidelong glance. Her profile could have been carved from granite.

She blew out a frustrated breath through her nose. "What is there to say, *alef*? You and Jax negotiated a heat contract. Somehow you dragged me into it as well, because apparently I'm an idiot. It was a nice few days. And then everything went to shit again, because that's what always happens."

"'*Nice*'?" I echoed skeptically. "That's the word you're going with?"

"Yes. It is. They're nice omegas. Having sex was nice. Everything was fucking *nice*, and now Beckett's gone and we're screwed."

I could feel her icy green glare on me without turning to look. She was trying to derail me... to get me thinking about Beckett instead of her issues. But the thing was, we couldn't do anything about Beckett until we got where we were going and talked to his contacts. Which meant there was no reason not to hash this out now, while we had the chance.

"Here's what I don't get," I said. "Leave Leona out of it for a minute, because I know that's a whole different can of worms as far as you're concerned. Let's talk about Kam instead. You can't mate him. You can't get him pregnant. You obviously like him. And you're still acting like it's Irina all over again. Why?"

There was a heavy pause.

I waited it out.

"You don't understand what it's like," she said eventually. "You have no conception of how it feels to lose an omega under your protection… to know that you've failed them, and to have their death on your conscience. I don't ever want you to learn what that feels like, *alef*. Either of you."

I thought about that for a few minutes.

"Okay. But what does you denying yourself have to do with that?" I asked. "Because watching you be miserable and alone isn't exactly convincing me and Jax not to go after those two while we have the chance."

Another pause.

"I—" Alex began, only to cut herself off. "I don't wish to discuss this now."

I snorted. "Yeah, I kind of got that part already."

"It's a distraction, and we can't afford distractions." Alex turned her head away, looking out the window. "Beckett's disappearance feels like an endgame scenario. For us, at least. Maybe even for the underground as a whole."

Personally, I would have been more than happy to focus on that distraction until we reached Montreal. Idly, I wondered if Jax was getting in some good *distractions*, alone in the remote safehouse with a pair of tempting omegas all to himself.

Lucky bastard.

Still, Alex had a point. Bravado aside, I understood that there was a good chance we weren't going to come out of this unscathed.

"You've really got no idea who Beckett's mate is, huh?" I asked. That was the part I kept coming back to—how much damage might be done if the wrong person managed to get their hands on that information.

"I really don't," Alex replied with a sigh. "And right now, I almost wish I did, just so I'd know how badly to panic."

We lapsed into silence as the outskirts of Montreal came into view.

<hr>

After some discussion, we'd decided to approach Beckett's contacts in the same order he'd intended to meet with them. He'd had three meetings planned, and we figured that if he hadn't made the first meeting, it was pretty much a given that he wouldn't have made it to the other two, either.

If he'd disappeared between one meeting and the next, it might at least give us some kind of a starting point in order to trace him. There'd been nothing in the newspapers so far indicating he'd been arrested. That could be good, or it could be bad. On the one hand, if he'd been scooped up and dumped into the legal system that would ultimately funnel him to the Committee's brutal parody of 'justice,' he was out of our reach and as good as dead. The underground didn't have the resources to go up against the Committee head-to-head — not even close. They'd crush us like bugs the moment we tried to crawl out of the wood-work.

On the other hand, it could be just as bad if Enoch Sloane had snatched Beckett in secret and was keeping him off the books for some reason — most likely so he and his lackeys would have time to extract every last bit of in-formation from him without the pressures of having to give him a sham trial. We also had the Beta Liberation Front assholes to consider. They might or might not be secretly working with the Committee. They also might or might not have their own reasons for wanting to take out the guy who'd singlehandedly busted up their operation in Romania.

Fuck, what a mess.

Beckett's first scheduled meeting had been with the go-between for another cell that was adjacent to ours. The guy was a beta, and he owned, of all things, a hair salon. We arrived to find the place empty and boarded up, the faded sign hanging off-kilter from a single chain above the locked door. That was our first hint that things might be even more serious than we'd thought.

"Keep driving," Alex said tightly. "Don't slow down."

I did, well aware that if the authorities had shut the shop down because of its ties with the underground, they might have surveillance in place to identify anyone who came poking around in search of the proprietor.

I continued for several miles before pulling into the parking lot of a run-down diner.

"It could be a coincidence," I said, though it almost certainly wasn't.

"I don't believe in coincidences," Alex replied. "But we don't have any way of knowing if the place was raided before or after Beckett showed up. Or even *if* he showed up."

"On to the next one?" I asked.

"On to the next one," she agreed.

The next meeting Beckett had scheduled was a step up the food chain, and as such, neither Alex nor I had contact details for a specific person. All we had was a location and a code phrase that would only be good for another day or two before it changed. The location was a large, well-known casino. Alex sent me in alone, since I was less conspicuous than a six-foot-tall butch female alpha would have been.

I double-checked my fake ID, tugged my suit jacket straight, and went inside. Once I got to the gaming floor, I searched out the pit boss and flagged her down. She was a beta woman with really big hair and a plastic smile.

"Can I help you?" she asked.

"Yeah, can you recommend a restaurant around here that does Ukranian food?" I asked.

She blinked at me. "Uh, that's... oddly specific. I think there's one downtown run by a family of Bulgarians. That's about the closest thing I know of." With that, she gave me another vacant smile and walked off.

It hadn't been the code response.

I found an empty blackjack table manned by a bored looking dealer and sat down to play. After I'd lost a bit of money, I jerked my chin toward the woman as she made the rounds through the various tables.

"New pit boss?" I asked. "I haven't seen her here before."

The dealer's uninterested eyes followed the gesture. "Oh, yeah. Not just her, either. New ownership came in last week and took a broom to the entire management team—swept 'em right out the door."

"Huh," I said. "That's pretty crazy. Hit me again, please."

He dealt me a six, for a total of eighteen.

"Stand," I said.

The dealer flipped over the hole card, revealing two tens.

After a couple more games, I tipped the guy and headed out.

"Well?" Alex asked, when I climbed into the Jeep and slammed the door shut.

"We're in the shit," I said without preamble. "Someone's taking out the underground in Montreal a piece at a time. They're cutting deep and fast. My guess is they must have inside knowledge."

―――――◆―――――

Beckett's third meeting was always going to be more of a challenge to deal with—another reason we'd put it off till last. This was the high-level stuff, where we assumed he'd been planning to discuss what Leo and Kam might be able to offer the underground thanks to the international diplomatic contacts they'd made over the years.

We didn't have a name. We didn't even have a location. Ironically, we might have been able to get that information from the person he'd intended to contact through the casino, but that approach was fucked, now.

"We need to go lower down the ladder, not higher," Alex said. "Find out what the foot soldiers know about the sweeps that are taking out the higher-ups."

I grunted acknowledgement. "Try The Jackal first?"

"Might as well start there," she agreed.

The Jackal was a dive bar at the edge of La Petite-Patrie, an unassuming working-class neighborhood situated south of Avenue Papineau and north of the railroad tracks. The owner wasn't a member of the underground as far as I knew, but she'd raised *not giving a shit about what her patrons got up to in her bar* to an art form. That made it a popular place for sympathizers to gather and discuss low-level business, and it meant we were likely to find a familiar face or two there.

The place was a squat brick building on the corner of two unremarkable streets, clinging like a grungy barnacle to a much larger building next to it. The neighborhood was a dump with cracks and potholes in the roads, not to mention a pervasive air of sketchiness. The view from the row of tiny, flyspecked windows along the side of the bar wall overlooked the loading dock at the back of a grocery store on the next block.

"You take me to all the nicest places," I told Alex. "Have I mentioned that lately?"

She shot me a glare and didn't reply.

Our entrance hadn't garnered much in the way of interest from the other patrons. The place was busy enough, with people getting off from their nine-to-five jobs and stopping by for a drink on their way home. I scanned the crowd, aware of Alex doing the same beside me. She touched my arm and jerked her chin toward a rat-faced man nursing a beer at the end of the bar.

His gaze flew up to us as we approached, his expression startled and wary. He looked vaguely familiar, but it wasn't anyone I knew personally. Alex apparently did, though.

"Étienne," she greeted.

The man's eyes grew wide. "Alex—what the *hell* are you doing here?"

"Good to see you, too," she said, deadpan. "I need information. Something big is going down, and we're out of the loop. We need to get back in the loop fast so we can figure out what's happening."

The guy looked like he was about to have an aneurysm. "What you need is to get the *fuck out of Montreal*. Are you crazy? Beckett got his name plastered all over the newspapers for breaking an unregistered omega out of police custody last month, and you're one of his alpha lapdogs. Think they're not after you, too?"

"Beckett's missing," Alex said flatly. "That's why we're here."

"Oh, *shit*." Étienne pushed his beer away. "How long has he been gone for?"

"A few days. He came to Montreal for a series of meetings and didn't come back when he was supposed to. Didn't leave a message with the usual go-between, either." Alex leaned closer. "We've been following a trail of busted businesses and casinos. What the hell is going on in this city?"

Étienne's eyes darted from side to side as though worried someone might be listening in, despite the loud buzz of conversation surrounding us. "It's been crazy for the last couple of weeks. Like, *batshit*. Every mid-level meeting place in the damned city has been hit with raids, and a lot of the higher ones, too. I almost stopped coming here to The Jackal in case they start dropping the hammer on the low-level joints, too—but it's the only way to get any news."

Alex exchanged a look with me before returning her attention to Étienne. "Is it just Montreal? Do you know? Or is this happening in other cities, too?"

He raised his hands in a helpless gesture. "No clue. The lines of communication have been cut. It's like we're under siege, and the longer it goes on the less information there is about what's happening."

There were wider implications, but only one that I was focused on right now. I tugged Alex to the side and lowered my voice, speaking close to her ear. "We're not gonna get anything useful about Beckett if everyone who might know something has already either been busted or made a run for it."

Alex was as tense as a drawn bowstring. Étienne gave a final nervous glance around the bar and rose to leave, looking like a man who would prefer to be pretty much anywhere else. Neither of us made a move to stop him.

"We need to get back to the others and reassess whether or not to cut our losses and find a different cell," Alex said. "If someone's got access to this level of information about the underground, it won't take long before the safehouse network is compromised, too."

The instinctual need to make sure Jax and the omegas were safe warred with my need to go after Beckett. I shoved the emotional turmoil aside, unwilling to deal with it.

"Okay," I said. "I'm not giving up on Beckett yet, though. Not until I know for sure that he's either dead or out of our reach for good."

Alex opened her mouth to say something, but the ambient hubbub of conversation in the bar rose abruptly in alarm. Several patrons surged to their feet, and others were crowding toward the line of grimy windows. The back of my neck prickled ominously.

"Trouble," I said unnecessarily.

Alex was already elbowing her way to one of the windows. I followed, shoving patrons out of the way until I could catch a glimpse outside, where half a dozen unmarked vans were parked across the street. Armed, black-clad figures spilled out of them in numbers that seemed ridiculous for a simple bar raid.

"*Fuck*," Alex cursed.

People were already scrambling for the exits — front and back. They were going to be met by a wall of armed police, though… assuming these were actually police and not something even more sinister.

Alex and I were both armed, but not with anything that would stand up to the kind of firepower on display outside.

"We fighting or what?" I asked, having to raise my voice over the increasing pandemonium of panicking patrons inside the bar.

"If anyone in here pulls a gun, they'll take it as an excuse to mow these people down," Alex shouted back. "Let's try to make for a back room, see if we can get behind their lines somehow and sneak out."

Assuming even a basic level of competence from the grunts outside, it wasn't a plan with a high likelihood of success—and she knew that as well as I did. Still, I scanned the interior looking for an employees-only door. Alex saw it first and pointed me in the right direction, just as the front door burst open and several small objects arced into the building.

Alex's hand closed convulsively on my arm, yanking me in the opposite direction.

"Stun grenades!" she cried, a moment before a wall of blinding light and deafening sound slammed into the crowd. I staggered and fell, the screaming that had started when the door opened cut off abruptly as my hearing went away.

ELEVEN

Jax

FLYNN AND ALEX hadn't returned, and the sense of watching a bad plan careening off the rails was becoming inescapable. There was still one more step to take before I transitioned into full-on panic mode. I'd need to check with Beckett's guy and make sure there wasn't a message waiting to explain why they were late. Then, if there wasn't one, I'd have to ask myself if I was going to abandon my pack, or if I was going to abandon the two omegas I was duty bound to protect—because it wouldn't be fair to drag Leona and Kam deeper into danger if I went after Alex and Flynn.

Kam and I were seated at the kitchen table. We had a clear line of sight to Leona, who was in the front room watching the driveway. This way, she could follow the conversation and keep an eye on things outside at the same time.

"Don't make your decision based on us," Kam was saying. "I know we'd be worse than useless in any kind of covert mission, especially with Leo's face plastered all over the news. We can stay in hiding while you do what you need to do—and if worse comes to worst, we could still buy our way out of the country if we had to."

He was trying to give me an out, and the scary part was, I might end up taking him up on it if there turned out to be no other option.

"What he said," Leona called from the other room. "My parents are hiding out under assumed identities in Jamaica. They'll help us, and if you and the others can make it there, I guarantee they'll help you and your pack, too. We could regroup and figure out what to do from there, where it's safer."

"We'll keep that option on the table," I said.

I'd wondered about her parents—she'd mentioned previously that she'd convinced them to leave the country for their own safety. They'd concealed their throwback child instead of turning her over to the Committee as they'd been legally bound to do, when she'd presented as an omega. Once her rise through the diplomatic corps had become meteoric, the danger to them became too great.

Ironically, one of the last things Leona and Kam had achieved in the diplomatic corps before Leo's arrest was the successful negotiation of a new treaty lessening the legal penalties for the so-called crime her parents had committed.

Whatever the case, I was glad to learn that they were well and evidently in a position to help her and Kam if things got really bad. I wasn't at all sure that getting out of the country would be as straightforward as Leona seemed to think, though. I guess it would depend on what kind of contacts they had access to in the underground. No unregistered omega got as far as they had without *some* kind of help, even if it was low-level stuff like acquiring pheromone suppressors.

Kam's fingers tapped against the tabletop in a nervous rhythm. "She's right that you should get out, too. And... the others."

There was a slight hesitation in the final words. I looked closer, and saw the hidden fear behind Kam's deep brown eyes. Like me, he expected the worst. He'd already written Beckett off, and he was bracing himself to do the same for the two alphas who hadn't returned to us when they said they would.

"I'm sure they just got held up and left a message with Beckett's contact," Leona said from the window. "It doesn't automatically mean something's gone wrong—it could mean they've found a lead."

There it was in a nutshell—her light to Kam's darkness. Yang to his yin. I wasn't sure if she really believed her own words, or if she was only trying to lighten the atmosphere of dread hanging over the room. To be fair, she might be absolutely right. Once upon a time, I probably would have assumed the best instead of the worst, too.

When the *hell* had that changed, anyway?

"Hopefully you're right," I said. "Whatever the case, I think we should find a new place to hide out. We've been here too long. We can leave a message for the others at the same time we're checking to see if they left one for us."

Kam shot Leona a speculative look. "Hmm. How do you feel about dyeing your hair, *odama*?"

She shot him a sour look. "Probably about the same as you'll feel about shaving off your beard, baby face."

He ran a hand over his short, anchor-style fringe of dark facial hair. "*Excuse me*. Do you have any idea how hard it is for an omega to grow a beard?"

"Sure," she called back. "I mean, I've heard you bitching about it often enough, right?"

They were trying to take my mind off things. Omega instinct, to comfort an upset alpha and defuse a tense situation. I wish I could say it was working.

God. Why could we not have met these two in a different world, where we could have courted them and mated them and had a *life*, instead of this constant barrage of slow-rolling crises?

"It's not the worst idea," I said, because honestly, that flaming red hair of hers *was* kind of hard to miss.

"So, we'll leave in the morning to meet with this message guy in Montreal?" Kam asked. "And buy hair dye."

"Right," I said, having no better plan. "As-suming the car's up to it, we can try for

Burlington afterward and hide out there for a bit. It's only a couple of hours' drive from Montreal, and there's a fair amount of anti-Committee sentiment brewing in Vermont. Might be safer."

Kam nodded.

"Sounds good," Leona agreed. "You know, as strange as it sounds, I'm going to miss this house."

It didn't sound strange at all. This was almost certainly the first place she'd ever stayed that had a proper omega nest, for one thing.

"If I were Flynn, I'd have some kind of crass joke at the ready regarding how memorable alpha dick is," I said, trying hard not to picture Flynn captured or dead, somewhere far out of my reach.

Kam gave a soft snort. "Well, to be fair, it *is* pretty memorable."

"There's certainly a decent amount of alpha dick tied up in my growing nostalgia for the place," Leona agreed solemnly.

I couldn't help a short laugh, despite the darkness surrounding us. For a few shining days, things had been idyllic. A pack house—though admittedly, a borrowed one—shared with people I'd happily spend the rest of my life with. Now, the question had once again become how short the rest of my life was likely to be.

"I'm honored that you chose to let us share your heat," I said. "And I know the others feel the same way."

Kam's eyebrows twitched upward a fraction. "What, even Alex?"

I gave him a sad smile. "You're the first omega she's been with since she lost her mate and pups years ago. That should tell you everything you need to know." I cleared my throat. "Anyway, take some time today and gather up everything you intend to take with us, but pack light. I'm going to see about dinner."

I got up to wrangle a decent meal for the three of us, hoping to make up for the fact that I'd left the bulk of the cooking to them over the past few days while I obsessed about the untenable security situation on the property. After making sure they were fed and set for the evening, I did a last circuit of the property line before dark, ensuring that all of the booby traps were still in place. Then I packed up my belongings and went to bed, determined to get a few hours of sleep before relieving Kam from his watch at three a.m.

I was somewhat successful in that endeavor, though my dreams were, to put it mildly, not the best. When I strapped on my shoulder and hip holsters and made my way quietly through the darkened house to the downstairs living room, it was to find that the two omegas had dragged the old sofa to a position in front of the window. Kam was seated near one end, dutifully keeping the watch, while Leona lay curled up against his side, wrapped in an afghan and fast asleep.

Kam glanced up at me as I approached, pausing in his rhythmic stroking of her fiery hair. I stopped, looking down at them—struck for the hundredth time by the picture they made together.

"Hi," Kam said softly. "I think we're both a bit on edge. Is it okay if we curl up here and help you stay awake by snoring at you?"

My heart clenched, falling victim yet again to the kryptonite these two seemed to possess.

"Always," I said.

"Thanks." Kam yawned, lifting the hand that wasn't cradling Leona to cover his mouth as he did. "Nothing to report, except a confused looking deer that wandered up a few hours ago and then bounded off in a huff. What time did you want to leave in the morning?"

"Let's say eight o'clock," I decided. "We can grab some breakfast first, and it should still give us plenty of time to get to Montreal, check in with Beckett's contact, and drive down to Burlington before dark."

"Assuming the Franken-Chrysler doesn't break down along the way," Kam said.

"I'm sure it will be fine," I told him, since I suspected that the car was going to be the least of our worries.

I was ridiculously and irrationally charmed by the fact that our quiet conversation hadn't caused Leona to so much as stir—though she did mumble a sleepy protest when Kam shuffled them around so he was lying full length on the couch with her body sprawled half on top of his. Giving into temptation, I settled into the small space left between the throw pillow Kam was using to support his head, and the sofa arm.

It provided a perfectly good view of the driveway, and had the added benefit of leaving both of them within easy reach. As I alternated stroking my right hand through first Leona's hair and then Kam's, the sweet aura of drowsy omegas leant me a fragile sense of peace as I contemplated what we might find tomorrow. Maybe Leona was right, and the others had found a promising lead on Beckett. Maybe we could still get him back and find a safe harbor somewhere. *Together.*

My thin veneer of serenity lasted for an hour or so, until the distant clatter of metal cans and plastic jugs on the far side of the house jerked my head around. Adrenaline flooded my system like an electric shock.

TWELVE

Jax

THE TWO omegas at my side were instantly awake, instinct pulling them from sleep in response to my sudden tension.

"What is it?" Leona asked, terror underlying her hoarse whisper.

It occurred to me what had happened to her the last time she'd been abruptly awoken from a sound sleep in the middle of the night. Unfortunately, I couldn't guarantee it wasn't about to happen again, even though whoever was outside would have to get past me to get to either of them.

"Something tripped one of the alarms," I said, rising to my feet. "Could be another wandering deer. Could be something worse."

Her eyes were very wide, luminous in the weak moonlight filtering through the trees outside.

"What should we do?" Kam asked quietly. He sounded more resigned than panicked.

"I need you to get the box of Molotov cocktails out of the storage room and soak the wicks with vodka." I pulled a lighter out of my pocket and handed it to him. "Leona, watch the driveway while I get to the other side of the house and check on the disturbance. Give a yell if you see anyone approaching from the front."

They both nodded their understanding. With a deep breath, I hurried off to see how much shit we were in, leaving them to get things prepped at the front of the house. Using the Molotovs in a wooded area like this was a gamble, but we were seriously low on options. There was no wind to speak of tonight, and I was banking on the surrounding forest being too damp to sustain the kind of fire that might blow back on us and burn down the house.

At best, the homemade firebombs might give anyone approaching second thoughts, while also illuminating the scene outside to give me a better view of my targets. At worst, they'd cause a bit more chaos than I could manage alone with just a pair of semiautomatic handguns.

I jogged through the house, my nerve-damaged left side complaining with every step. My head ached a bit more than usual tonight, not helped by the current adrenaline dump.

Suck it up, buttercup. I could almost hear Flynn's voice in my ear. As long as my vision didn't start swimming badly enough to affect my aim, I'd deal with it.

The safehouse had security lights on each of the outside walls, but we'd kept them off to avoid attention from anyone who might have a clear line of sight to the house at night. No point in advertising our presence here, after all.

Now, however, I charged into the dining room on the side of the house where the noise had come from and switched on the exterior floodlight. It illuminated the woods beyond the grassy side yard, throwing crazy shadows among the branches and tree trunks.

Some of those shadows were moving.

"*Fuck*," I breathed.

We'd left the window open, to make listening for noise coming from outside easier. Standing to one side, out of the line of fire, I pulled the gun from my shoulder holster, checked the clip, and loosed a shot in the direction of the movement among the trees. I held out very little hope of hitting anything through the confusion of trees and underbrush, but getting confirmation that we were armed and aware of their approach might at least slow our attackers down and make them rethink their strategy.

I ducked behind the cover of the wall again, waiting to see if there'd be any immediate return fire. There wasn't.

Leona slipped into the room a few moments later. I waved at her to stay out of any potential line of sight from outside. She crouched low and skirted the wall to approach me.

"There are people moving around in front, and also on the west side of the house," she said. Her voice was shaking. "The east side is so overgrown that it's difficult to tell, but there may be some there, too. It's hard to see how many there are, exactly, but… well… it's a lot."

We were in trouble, and she knew it.

"The moment anyone leaves the tree line, you lob a Molotov at them," I said, just as another clatter of tin cans came from the woods to the west. "I'll try to keep them busy here and on the east side. They haven't fired on us yet, but there's no question they'll be armed. Stay away from the windows except to hurl bottles at them."

"Jax," she said quietly. "There are too many. The three of us won't be able to fight them off by ourselves."

"If they get in, you and Kam run upstairs to the nest," I said, not answering her directly. "I'll try to hold them at the bottom of the stairs."

She gave me a heartbroken look, and it was fucking Romania all over again—knowing that all I could do was die for them, and it still wouldn't be enough. I could tell she wanted to argue with me. Instead, she reached up and grasped the back of my neck, pulling me down for a brief kiss.

"All right," she whispered, her voice husky with emotion. "Thank you, Jax."

My throat tried to close up, but we didn't have time for that kind of shit.

"Go," I managed. "Throw a few bottles at them and make them think twice about leaving the trees."

With a hesitant nod, she retraced her steps along the wall and ducked out, returning to her *odama* at the front of the house. I shoved every emotion except cold anger down into the deep, dark pit behind my ribs, and snuck another look out of the corner of the window. The shadows seemed closer, so I let off another shot—painfully aware that my supply of ammunition was far from bottomless.

It was barely two minutes later when several things happened at once. I smelled burning cloth, and heard Kam's grunt of effort as he presumably hurled the first Molotov cocktail out of the window. The muted crash of breaking glass and a distant roar of flames outside coincided with a high-intensity spotlight flaring into life at the edge of the tree line, directed right into the window I was peering out of.

The dazzling light blinded me, obscuring what was going on behind it. I cursed sharply and lifted my gun, trying to aim for the source and take it out. It took four shots before I heard the crash of something shattering and the spotlight went dark, leaving me blinking away afterimages. Before I could clear my vision, a second, identical light came on, every bit as powerful as the first. My headache pounded with renewed viciousness in response. I clenched my jaw against the pain and sent half a dozen more shots out the window—all without obvious effect.

Staggering away, I kept a hand on the wall in an effort not to run into anything, and headed for the east side of the house to try and discourage the ones on that side from getting too cocky. I arrived to find the same thing there—multiple high-intensity lights playing over the house in a blinding onslaught that made it impossible to get a bead on the approaching forces. I shot a few rounds at them anyway and succeeded in taking out one light—but it didn't make much difference with others still drilling holes through my skull.

From the sounds of it, Kam and Leo were still lobbing Molotovs—though I had little doubt they were facing similar conditions. I headed to the living room to grab a few of the gasoline-filled bottles for myself, figuring they might end up being a more effective weapon at this point.

A metallic clanking noise came from elsewhere in the house, like something had hit the floor and rolled. It sounded as though it had come from the dining room, and all the tiny hairs on the back of my neck stood up in unison. A low hissing noise followed a second later.

"Fuck!" I charged back to the room. I could barely fucking see with the brutal light coming from outside, but the sound of escaping gas was enough to guide me to a small canister on the floor. Holding my breath, I scooped it up and hurled it out the same window it had just come through.

Around the house, more clunks sounded, followed by more hissing. A second canister arced through the dining room window and skittered against the wall. I scrambled for it, getting a face full of pale, odorless gas as it hissed into life before I could toss it outside with the other one.

Rather than wait around, I stumbled toward the front room in search of Leona and Kam, uncomfortably aware of the faint numbness settling over my extremities after even such a brief exposure to whatever the fuck was in those devices. I absolutely refused to think about the VX nerve agent derivative the terrorists had been working on. Right now, all that mattered was making sure the omegas got away from it.

I slid to a halt in the doorway to find Kam slamming an upside down wastebasket over one canister, while Leona lunged for one sitting in the corner and threw it outside. There were more of them in the other rooms, too—the crazy beams of blinding light from outside illuminated wisps of white vapor rolling along the floor like someone had switched on a Hollywood fog machine inside the house.

Another canister clattered into the living room and ricocheted off the wall, sliding under the sofa and bursting into hissing life.

"Get upstairs!" I ordered, appalled to find that my words were slurring. "Keep th' windows closed so they can't throw any into the second floor. I'll clear these out!"

Vapor streamed from beneath the upended trashcan. Leona—who'd been tugging fruitlessly at one corner of the sofa in an attempt to get to the other one—fell to one knee, coughing. Kam and I lunged for her in unison.

"Get her out!" I ordered, pressing her into Kam's arms and grabbing the sofa myself. He staggered in the direction of the staircase as I shoved the offending furniture away and tried to feel around through the growing cloud of gas for the source of the hissing. The air in the room was growing hazy, and I could barely make out the pair going down in a tangle of limbs just before they reached the doorway.

"*Jax!*" Kam's hoarse cry dissolved into coughing.

He sounded like he was shouting down a long tunnel, even though he was barely fifteen feet away. My clumsy fingers bumped against a metallic casing. When I tried to pick it up so I could throw it away, the whole floor came along with it and slammed me unceremoniously in the face.

I lay on the hardwood, disoriented—trying to remember which way was up so I could get my damned face out of the gas. Despite my efforts to push my body upright with my arms, nothing happened. Distantly, I heard the sound of men shouting orders outside. Boots pounded across gravel, but it might as well have been happening on a different planet as far as my brain was concerned.

Maybe if I just close my eyes for a second, I thought. *Just to regroup…*

I didn't open them again.

THIRTEEN

Leona

I WOKE UP with a pounding headache and my tongue stuck to the roof of my mouth. An unpleasantly hazy blank space separated my memories of the recent past—searchlights blinding me as hissing metal canisters flew through the windows—from wherever the hell I was now.

There was a kind of strange hissing background noise here, too—but it was different than before. More of a low drone. *Airplane,* my brain identified helpfully. I pried sticky eyelids open. It felt like dragging sandpaper across my eyeballs, and I could only see blurry shapes without detail. To make matters even more unpleasant, I desperately needed to use the restroom.

A soft groan of distress escaped my lips. I would have committed murder for a glass of water.

"Leo?" Kam's soft rasp cut through my confusion like a razor blade. It sliced through my numbness to release the cold terror that I'd forgotten about in my drugged haze.

I made another wordless noise and reached in the direction his voice had come from. My arm jerked to a halt, unyielding metal digging into my wrist. I pulled fitfully against the restraint. Metal clinked against metal.

"You're handcuffed to the seat," Kam said hoarsely. "We both are. We're on a plane—flying south, I think. Are you all right?"

More memories crowded in. Dear god—*the gas canisters*. I'd thought they'd used the nerve agent on us… that we were all as good as dead.

"We're alive?" I croaked. It came out sounding like a question. I tried to reach for him again, only to remember the handcuff when it pulled me up short. I lifted the other arm instead, reaching awkwardly across my body. Chilly fingers tangled with mine and squeezed.

"For the moment, we are," Kam replied.

I blinked rapidly, desperate to get some moisture in my eyes. "Jax?" I asked, dreading the answer.

"Here," came the tight reply.

Tears of relief at the proof that all three of us had survived finally allowed me to lubricate my eyeballs, and blink my surroundings into some kind of focus. We were on a mid-sized turboprop plane, based on the engine noise. It was daytime. Kam and I were each handcuffed to our metal seat frames by our right wrists, with our left arms free. Jax, by contrast, was shackled hand and foot, his muscles bulging as he strained against his bondage.

We were at the front of the plane—Kam next to me in the window seat, with Jax across the aisle from us. I craned to look behind me and found a good two dozen stony-faced military or paramilitary types watching us fixedly. My stomach dropped.

One of them unbuckled his seatbelt and rose, approaching us. He stopped and looked down at me for a moment before extending a canteen toward me. An angry red burn mark covered his right cheekbone—a few blisters decorating the center, and the eyebrow on that side half singed away.

"Drink," he said, in a heavily accented voice.

Russian? From the heavy vowel and the way he swallowed the '*k*,' I thought it must be.

I let go of my grip on Kam and took the canteen cautiously, holding it with my free hand so I could unscrew the top with my cuffed hand. The water was lukewarm but seemed fresh, so I drank cautiously—cognizant of the current state of my bladder.

The fear was going to hit me properly any time now. There was only one thing this could mean—we'd been captured by the Committee. And yet... aspects of the situation felt *off*, somehow.

I offered the canteen to Kam. He shook his head, so I capped it again and handed it back to the soldier.

"Thank you," I told him, trying to feel out the situation a bit more. "May I ask whose custody we're in?"

The part of me that remembered being dragged out of my apartment in the middle of the night wanted to cringe back in fear, expecting a blow in retaliation for my question. But my higher brain functions were still rebooting—not quite on board with the program yet. It allowed me to pretend this wasn't what it realistically had to be, and let me act with a level of courage and detachment I probably wouldn't have been capable of displaying otherwise.

"You are prisoners of the Euro-Soviet branch of the Committee on Alphomic Suppression, *malyshka*," he said. I'd been right—there was no mistaking his Russian accent. "Be glad you did not succeed in killing any of my men, or this flight might have been much less pleasant for everyone involved."

Jax jerked sharply against one of his wrist shackles, the seat frame creaking with strain. It was pretty clear he'd have been happy to take his chances with that.

"Where are you taking us?" Kam asked, trying his luck since the soldier seemed willing to talk.

"That is not your concern," the man said.

"Why the Euro-Soviet branch, though?" I pressed, desperately attempting to get some more brain cells firing. "Why not the North

American branch? Aren't we outside your jurisdiction?"

The man gave a thin smile that twisted with discomfort when it pulled at his burn injury. I wondered which of our Molotov cocktails had been the one to get him.

"Not for much longer," he said.

That was unhelpfully cryptic. Practicality raised its head before I ended up making him angry or driving him back to his seat.

"I really need to use the bathroom. Is that allowed?" I asked, doing my best to look unthreatening. Not a stretch, really.

He beckoned to another of the soldiers, who came and joined him in the aisle. The second man removed a small keychain from his pocket and leaned down, unlatching my cuffs.

I rubbed at my wrist, rising on wobbly legs as the new soldier stepped back to give me space. He gestured toward the rear of the plane.

Jax rattled his cuffs again. "Touch her, and I'll see you dead, even if I have to crash this plane to do it," he said, his tone murderous.

It hit me rather abruptly that Jax was... *not okay*. Which, I mean, *fair enough*. None of us were okay. I was still functioning because the situation hadn't hit me properly yet. And Kam only went to pieces *after* a crisis; never *during* a crisis.

"It's all right," I told Jax softly, begging him with my eyes not to provoke our captors.

"If they wanted to hurt us, they'd have done it already."

This was the Committee, after all. The torture and death would come later.

The thought sent my balance slewing sideways for a second. I grasped the chair back and steadied myself, allowing the soldier who'd uncuffed me to usher me past the rows of uniformed beta males. Their eyes were a heavy weight on me, but none of them raised a hand or spoke a word as I squeezed past them in the narrow aisle.

The bathroom was barely big enough to sit down, and my guard didn't blink an eye when I closed the door and engaged the privacy lock. When I was done, I washed my hands and splashed water on my face from the tiny sink, then straightened my shoulders and exited. The guard led me back to my seat, where the man with the burned face still stood watch over Jax and Kam. Once I was handcuffed again, they both left, returning to their seats without a word.

"This doesn't make sense," Kam said in a low voice.

There was little doubt that the closest soldiers would be able to hear us, but they didn't show any indication that they cared whether we talked to each other or not.

"No," I agreed. "It should have been Enoch Sloane's operation. Why is the Euro-Soviet branch poaching on UFNA territory?"

"Turf wars," Jax muttered, still looking like he'd enjoy nothing better than getting free and ripping out some spines.

I traded a considering glance with Kam. It was an open secret that Kostya Nikolayev, the head of the Euro-Soviet branch, was locked in a power struggle with Enoch Sloane.

"Maybe," I allowed.

"Too bad that doesn't really help us," Kam said.

Unfortunately, I had to agree with him.

———————◆———————

When the plane finally banked some time later, making a final approach for landing, Kam peered through the window, craning to look down. "That's Cuba, I'm pretty sure," he said, his brow furrowing. "We passed over the Florida Keys not long ago."

I stretched, crowding against him to get a look as well. Based on the long, narrow shape of the island, he was right. We were heading for the one of the southeastern provinces—a green and mountainous stretch of land. With a sudden ache in my heart, I realized that I was, at this moment, only five hundred miles or so away from my parents in Kingston—separated by nothing but a tiny expanse of salt water.

Hi, Mom and Dad.

Bye, Mom and Dad.

"Cuba has strong Russian ties," Jax said.

"Makes sense," I replied. The island nation had so far managed to avoid being snapped up by the United Federation of North America as either a territory or a protectorate. They'd done that by playing footsie with the Soviets, who were more than happy to have an ally located a scant hundred miles off the coastline of their rival on the world stage.

My insides rose unpleasantly as the plane shed altitude. The runway where we eventually touched down was a bit bumpy, but serviceable—obviously a private airfield, though an expensive one based on the size. Mountain slopes draped in vibrant green tropical forest vegetation surrounded the narrow valley containing the airstrip. The plane taxied to a stop in front of a hangar with corrugated metal siding, where several black, official looking vehicles waited next to an army truck with canvas covering the back.

The sound of the men behind us unlatching their seatbelts dragged my attention away from the window. Four of them approached us, including the two who'd been up here earlier to give me water and take me to the bathroom.

"This is what will happen next," said the one who seemed to be in charge. His eyes settled on Jax. "You will all be taken to a vehicle and transferred to a holding facility for processing. Two guards will escort your omega companions, with guns trained on them the whole time. If you attempt to resist or escape, they will shoot. Do you understand?"

"Yes," Jax said, his eyes promising bloody vengeance at some unspecified future date.

My heart sped up, tripping over itself at the thought that we would soon be separated. And then, the real horrors would begin. The panic that had been lurking beneath the surface of my thoughts rippled, threatening to surge up and swallow me.

Would it be better to end it here? To fight back, and provoke them into shooting all three of us? But... I couldn't watch as Kam and Jax were shot down, their lives bleeding onto the ground in front of me. I *couldn't*.

And there was also the mystery behind the Euro-Soviets' interference. Why them, and not Sloane's men? Why *Cuba*? It didn't make any sense, and part of me was desperate to solve the puzzle. As horrified as I was at the thought of being separated from the others, at least then I wouldn't have to watch them suffer... or die. Just like they wouldn't have to watch me suffer and die.

We had a little more time until I had to let them go. We had the vehicle ride to this *holding facility*.

Two guards unhooked Jax's shackles and urged him to his feet at gunpoint. I stood up when my guard indicated I should, trying to control my trembling as a gun barrel pressed lightly against my back. Behind me, I heard Kam rise as well. We trooped out of the cabin, and descended a portable staircase that had been rolled into place at the plane's entrance.

The sun was dazzling. It was a perfectly warm, balmy tropical day. A faint breeze rustled my hair. The air smelled of damp earth and growing things, marred slightly by the exhaust from the plane and the parked vehicles.

Our guards directed us toward the back of the military truck.

"Get in," said Kam's guard.

Kam found a hand and foothold and clambered into the covered truck bed, his guard following right behind.

"You, too," said the man behind me, nudging me with the gun.

I was still shaky with emotional reaction — not to mention the dregs of the tranquilizing gas — but I managed to climb in after a couple of clumsy false starts. There was a space on the bench next to Kam, and neither of the guards protested when I took it, my thigh pressing against my *odama*'s. They didn't protest when I took his hand, either, curling our fingers together for comfort. The second guard merely sat down on my other side, the pair of them hemming us in, guns still trained on us.

Jax entered, favoring his left side heavily.

"Sit there," said one of the guards, indicating the bench against the opposite side of the truck bed from us. The alpha complied, warily assessing our situation, and was promptly flanked by his two armed guards.

The vehicle jerked into motion, jouncing and swaying. I considered trying to engage the soldiers in conversation in an attempt to get more information, but the engine rumbled loudly and the air in the covered bed stank of diesel exhaust. Besides, what did I truly expect to accomplish? These men were hired muscle, nothing more—even if they'd showed more restraint in their dealings with us than I might have expected.

I squeezed Kam's hand tighter and leaned against him, staying silent.

The weight of Jax's bloodshot blue gaze rested on me heavily. I met his eyes, even though doing so was painful. He glanced away, but not before I saw the fear lurking in his expression. A moment later, our gazes connected again, and he let me see his silent apology for not somehow magically having prevented all of this.

He was alone, separated from his pack and sick with worry over their safety. For the second time in only a handful of months, he'd been thrust into the role of sole protector to two omegas, pitted against overwhelming odds. This time, his failure would certainly mean his death... but that wasn't the part that was eating him up.

It was us. Kam and me.

We wouldn't have wanted anyone else as a protector, I tried to convey wordlessly. Maybe I should have gathered my courage and said it aloud, but the idea of giving these beta Committee soldiers a glimpse into something so personal was unbearable.

The journey dragged, though it probably didn't last more than twenty minutes in reality. I spent it pressing my body as closely as I could against Kam's — trying to ignore the guns pointed at us. Instead, I watched the thoughts and regrets scull behind Jax's eyes like clouds against a brilliant summer sky.

The unpleasant judder of bad roads and worn suspension eased to something smoother. Paved, I was fairly sure. We couldn't see anything with the canvas pulled across the opening in the back, but I sensed we were close to our destination. I soaked in the presence of the others, not knowing when I might need these final memories of closeness to hold a worse reality at bay.

The truck rolled to a stop with a high-pitched squeal of brakes, and a fresh puff of diesel exhaust made my nose wrinkle. One of Jax's guards pulled the canvas flap covering the opening aside.

As perfunctorily as they'd ordered us into the truck, the soldiers ushered us down from the bed. I swayed, my knees threatening to give way, but the man guarding me steadied me with one hand.

I looked around, taking in our surroundings. We were on some kind of private estate. The area was every bit as secluded as the airstrip had been. There was a massive house in the Colonial style of architecture standing nearby, its exterior white and gleaming in the afternoon light. Our escorts herded us toward a large outbuilding. While not nearly as ornate, it appeared to be of the same solid brick and stone construction as the house.

Holding facility, the lead guard had said.

This wasn't what I'd pictured, but it would be every bit as inescapable as a prison. For one thing, there was nowhere to run except into the endless mountain forests. And even that much would be a stretch—dozens of uniformed guards patrolled the property with high-powered rifles slung over their shoulders.

It was likely the Committee had properties like this one scattered across the world. With a chill, I wondered what horrors lay within the square outbuilding with its small, high windows and plain white facade.

We found out soon enough. The main entrance opened onto a guard station, which wasn't unexpected. There, we were handed off to new guards led by a slender woman with a military cap pulled low on her forehead, the bill throwing her face into shadow. She and her underlings were armed, and every bit as no-nonsense as the soldiers on the plane had been.

I noticed Jax giving the woman an odd look—perhaps surprised to find a female in a position of power within the reactionary ranks of the Committee. The male guards prodded us into motion, ushering us down a hallway and through an electronic security door. Beyond lay a second doorway. It was vaguely reminiscent of the thick metal cell door in the terrorist cave in Romania, and I couldn't suppress a shiver.

When the woman opened it, however, the room beyond appeared to be a basic but pleasant living space with a decently sized bed, table, chairs, sink, toilet, and even a homey rug covering the concrete floor. I blinked in confusion.

"In," said the woman in a light Russian accent, and Jax pierced her with another long stare.

"All three of us?" Kam asked hesitantly.

"Yes," she said. "Move."

We entered, having little choice since the security door behind us was already closed. The woman drew her sidearm but kept it pointed at the ground.

She jerked her head toward the table and chairs. "Sit."

Cautiously, we crossed and did as we were told. I locked eyes with Kam—his left shoulder lifted in a bewildered shrug. Once we were seated, she turned to her subordinates.

"Close the door and wait outside," she ordered in a clear tone of command.

The men left without question, closing the door behind them and leaving us alone with the woman. She regarded us from beneath her cap, face still in shadow.

"Be aware that if you were to succeed in overpowering me—which is doubtful—it would not help you escape this room." She stepped back to lean her shoulders against the wall. "And now, we will talk."

"Show us your face," Jax rasped. "*Show me your face*, damn it."

Full, red lips twitched beneath the cap's shadow. The woman lifted a hand to tug it free, the gun in her other hand never wavering. Honey blonde hair swept up in a practical chignon topped a pixie-like face with large gray eyes. I heard Jax draw in a sharp breath. Kam and I traded a brief, mystified look.

"*Irina*," Jax breathed, barely the shape of a word.

Irina smiled, sharp and sibylline. "Hello, Jax. Fancy meeting you here."

FOURTEEN

Leona

KAM AND I gaped at them. *Irina*? As in, *Alex's* Irina? What the actual... *what*? Of course, Jax looked every bit as gobsmacked as I felt. Maybe even more so.

"You... you're... not dead?" he choked out, at more of a loss than I'd ever seen him before. In the next instant, anger slid over his pleasant features. "And you're working for *them*?"

Not just anger. Rage. It dripped from every pore.

Irina raised an eyebrow. "No, Jax—I've cunningly infiltrated their operation over the course of several years, and now I've randomly decided to blow my own cover by talking to someone who can identify me. I know you've had a rough day, but do at least *try* to use your fucking brain."

A low, menacing growl rumbled through Jax's chest.

"Excuse me," I said, rising from the table and stepping in front of Jax before alpha rage could get the better of him. Kam mirrored me, and between us we cut the woman off from his line of sight. "It's pretty clear there are some undercurrents here I don't understand, but for now, maybe you can tell me why we're in Euro-Soviet custody after an operation that took place inside UFNA territory."

"Oh good," Irina said. "Someone's still using their brain, at least."

"Chairman Nikolayev and Chairman Sloane have a very public feud," Kam suggested. "And Leona McCready is a high-profile fugitive. Catching her seems like it would be something of a coup in PR terms."

"*Two* people using their brains," Irina said. "Even better! But no, that's not it."

"Then what?" Jax snarled. I glanced back to find him gripping the edge of the table with an intensity that might splinter the wood at any moment.

"Enoch Sloane has Rhys Beckett," Irina said simply. "And *that* is a serious problem for everyone."

My heart sank, even though Beckett's capture by the Committee had always been the most likely scenario to explain his disappearance.

"Why is it a problem?" Kam asked cautiously. "Again, it seems as though it would be a cause for celebration among the Committee higher-ups."

"You might think so," Irina agreed, grim-faced. "But here's the thing—Sloane isn't running him through the usual channels. He's keeping Beckett off the books. And now, we have reason to think Sloane has also acquired effective leverage to use against him."

"Leverage," I echoed, my stomach joining my heart in free fall. "What does that mean, exactly?"

"It means Sloane's got Alex and Flynn as well," Jax grated. "And he thinks he can use them to crack Beckett wide open. *Fuck.*"

Irina met my eyes. "Sloane wants the identity of Beckett's mate. It's absolutely vital that he doesn't get it."

A fresh jolt of disquiet tightened my shoulders at the casual way Irina had thrown that little-known fact at our feet. The idea that Beckett's omega status was apparently common knowledge inside the Committee was bad enough. That they also knew about the existence of his secret mate seemed inconceivable.

"So Nikolayev wants the information instead?" I asked, still trying to arrange these puzzle pieces into something that made sense, when all I really wanted to do was crawl into a corner and rock mindlessly back and forth for a bit.

"Sloane will use the information like a wrecking ball, not caring what's destroyed in the course of his jihad," Irina replied. "Nikolayev moved to ensure that Sloane didn't get hold of you, too. Not that it will matter in the end, if Sloane is able to achieve what he wants using the tools he already has."

"And by tools—"

Jax grunted and cut me off. "She means Flynn and Alex." I glanced over my shoulder in time to see him shoot Irina a look of pure hatred.

There was a faint pause, and then Kam asked, "How did Nikolayev discover the location of the safehouse where we were staying?"

It was a good point. If Sloane had tortured the information out of Beckett, that would at least have made sense. But how would *Nikolayev* have gained access to that kind of closely guarded knowledge?

"He knows all sorts of things you might not expect him to," Irina said. "It's kind of his thing."

"I want to talk to him," I said impulsively. It was half a lie—I did not, in fact, want to face the terrifying Committee chairman, especially as his prisoner.

His… strangely well-treated prisoner.

But Nikolayev was a reptile, whereas Sloane was a rabid dog. My rational mind screamed that they were equally dangerous— just in different ways. But my instincts remembered the cold-blooded concessions Nikolayev had made to me at the summit. He understood the necessity of give-and-take when larger things were at stake. He was *rational*.

At least, he was rational if you ignored the stories about what he'd done to his throwback sister, and the fact that he'd allegedly enjoyed hunting omegas like animals for sport when he was younger. Gooseflesh prickled over my body, despite the fact that the cell was pleasantly warm.

"The chairman is already on his way here," Irina said. "I've no doubt he'll want to talk to you, too."

Great. *There* was a conversation to look forward to. Be careful what you ask for...

"Tell me something, traitor," Jax said, in a low, dangerous tone. "Since you're still alive, what about the pups? Alex's pups?"

Irina went very still for a moment. Her voice grew thin and distant as she said, "They're dead and burned to ash, torn from my body... just like our mating bond." Then she blinked free of her momentary reverie. "I will leave you now. Food and drink will arrive shortly. After that, you have my word that you will not be disturbed until morning."

With that, she turned her back on us and left the cell. The sound of the lock clicking into place echoed behind her.

———————◆———————

The food came as promised. We ate it, because that seemed like a better decision than not eating it and being hungry. It wasn't drugged. It wasn't even disgusting slop. Large parts of the current situation still didn't make sense.

Additionally, Jax was losing it. With his boss and packmates captured and quite possibly undergoing torture at Enoch Sloane's hands, the three of us in Committee custody, and a ghost from the past haunting him, our kindhearted alpha had finally reached capacity.

"It's crazy," he said, pacing back and forth across the cell with hitching, uneven strides. He scrubbed a hand through his close-cropped blond hair, ruffling it. "This is *crazy*. Why would she work for them after what they did to her?"

"How certain are you that she's telling the truth about the pups?" I asked, hating that there was even a question about it.

It was Kam who answered. He was sprawled on the bed, rumpled and obviously exhausted. "If Alex felt the bond break, the only possibility I can see is that they cut out Irina's mating gland. And if that's the case, it's unlikely the pregnancy could have continued to term, even if they didn't sterilize her at the same time. The hormonal disruption would have been too much."

Jax growled, and didn't pause in his restless pacing. "Right. So they mutilated her, killed her pups, and now she's acting like Nikolayev's pet lapdog? That's even worse."

I tapped a fingernail against the table. "Why is she alive at all? She was an unregistered omega openly infiltrating the beta military. She should be dead."

"Another good point," Kam agreed.

"And once again, she was captured in the UFNA, but here she is with the Euro-Soviets." I sighed. "If we were free and we still had our positions at the Foreign Office, we could at least dig into the court records. Find out what her official fate was supposed to be."

"If we were free, we could do a lot of things," Jax said, frustration rolling off him in waves.

"As much as we might wonder what's going through Irina's head, there's another angle I don't get," I mused. "What's the value in keeping her? From Nikolayev's perspective, I mean? She's an omega. Yes, she was in the beta military, but only on the admin side, right?"

"Yeah," Jax confirmed.

"So what makes a brainwashed omega valuable enough for him to not only keep her alive, but put her in a position of authority over beta soldiers?" I glanced between my two companions. "Why not use a brainwashed alpha instead? Or, for that matter, just use betas since the entire point of the organization is to get rid of alphas and omegas?"

"Omegas can be fighters, too," Kam said quietly. "It's a different skill set—speed and flexibility rather than brute strength. Just look at Beckett. But you're right, in the context of the Committee, it doesn't make a lot of sense."

Jax came to an abrupt halt in the center of the room. His eyes bored into me. "I don't want you alone with Nikolayev." His blue gaze played over Kam as well. "Either of you."

I didn't want to be alone with Nikolayev either, but my wants—and Jax's—didn't really come into it at this point.

"Jax," I said, as calmly as I could manage. "We're prisoners. As much as I appreciate having you here, you can't protect us now."

That was probably a harsh thing to say to an alpha—confirmed when Jax snapped, "*You think I don't know that?*" with a whipcrack of alpha bark in the words.

Kam and I flinched in unison. Jax froze, his shoulders a rigid line of tension.

"I'm sorry," he breathed. "Shit—I'm sorry. I didn't mean to bark."

I forced myself to relax, unclenching my muscles one by one. "We know. It's okay. We're all on edge."

He seemed to deflate, pulling out the chair across from me and sinking into it. He put his elbows on the table and scrubbed the heels of his hands against his eye sockets before looking up with a sigh.

"You know what I can't stop thinking about?" he asked.

"What?" I said.

He blew out a sharp breath. "If we were all mated, I'd at least be able to tell if Alex and Flynn are okay. If they're in pain, or..." He trailed off and shook his head.

"They're almost certainly not *okay*," Kam said, quietly brutal. "Knowing what Alex went through with Irina, would you really want a front-row seat for whatever's happening to them?"

Jax was silent for a long moment.

"Yes," he said hoarsely, and just like that, the fragile bravado that had sustained me up to this point fled. I wanted to cling to him and cry.

"We're in a cell inside a remote compound in rural Cuba," Kam went on. "We've been given assurances that no one will disturb us until morning. That might be true or it might be false, but in the end, I'm not sure it really matters. There is quite literally nothing productive we can do until Nikolayev or someone else in power shows up to talk with us. I, for one, have no desire to huddle on this bed alone while you two stay up all night exhausting yourselves with what-ifs. So would both of you please come over here and ensure I don't have to do that?"

I wiped away a stray tear that escaped my shaky control. We'd been given the gift of one more night together, even if we were missing some of the people who should have been here with us. Tomorrow was shrouded in a fog of uncertainty. Tonight might be all we had left.

Rising from the table, I held my hand out to Jax. After the smallest of hesitations, he took it.

"We're making a habit of this," I told him, leading him toward the bed. "The three of us stuck in a cell together."

"At least this time you can hold us properly, instead of sitting against the far wall with your dick out," Kam put in. "The lack of untreated shrapnel wounds is a nice touch, too."

I dropped Jax's hand and toed off my shoes. The alpha pinched the bridge of his nose and let out a pained huff that might have been distantly related to a self-deprecating laugh.

"And I still can't do a damned thing to keep you safe," he said. "It's like déjà vu all over again."

Kam shrugged. "If it makes you feel better, we can't do a damned thing to keep you safe, either. Life sucks."

And then you die, I finished silently.

Jax raised an eyebrow at Kam. "You're a real barrel of sunshine, you know."

"That's me," he agreed.

"He's loads of fun at parties," I said, trying to lighten the mood. "You know, he once accidentally-on-purpose spilled a gin and tonic down my cleavage at a Foreign Office Christmas party, when we were competing for the same internship."

Kam scowled at me. "That's a gross mischaracterization and you know it."

I shoved Jax into the center of the bed, pleased that he was distracted enough to allow it.

"All right, fine," I said, squeezing in on Jax's other side. "You only did it because my pheromone suppressor gave out early and you were trying to hide my scent before any of the betas noticed. Details, details."

"I didn't even want that internship!" Kam protested. "They were trying to foist it on me. I was *more* than happy to let you have it."

"'*Let*'?" I echoed, leaning into the banter even as I leaned into Jax's side, curling a leg over his and reaching across his chest to tangle my hand with Kam's. "You '*let*' me have it?"

"Yes," Kam said emphatically, mirroring my position on Jax's other side. "I *let* you have it. You're fabulous, Leo—but you had no idea how to employ omega wiles back then. Seriously—*none*."

Jax's arms came around our shoulders and tightened. "You're both using them now. On me."

I gazed up at him from beneath lowered lashes. "Is it working?"

He tugged me up far enough that he could press a kiss to my temple, and then my lips. Warmth crept through me from the point of contact, banishing some of the chill of fear that had been clinging to me. I watched as he pulled away and repeated the action with Kam, his movements tentative.

It occurred to me that this might well be the first time they'd kissed. Some of my memories were hazy, but I was pretty sure Flynn and Alex had been the ones to monopolize Kam during my heat.

Kam's eyes fluttered closed, and his free hand came up to brush Jax's cheek lightly. The stress-soured scent of Jax's woodsy pheromones sweetened into musky arousal between us, and I felt an answering sensation of liquid heaviness growing within the cradle of my pelvis.

Maybe it was reckless since we had no real assurance that Irina had been telling the truth, but if this was to be our last night of privacy and togetherness, my body knew *exactly* how I wanted to spend it.

FIFTEEN

Kam

IN THE END, my life had ended up far better than I could ever have expected. Mere hours ago, I'd thought I was about to join Leo and Jax as the first official victims of an experimental nerve gas. Even after waking up, the most likely scenario had seemed to involve a fate far less pleasant than being locked in a comfortable room with my packmate and a friendly alpha.

Jax was in some ways a very straightforward man, and in others, a difficult one to read. He'd kept his distance with me, at least compared to Alex and Flynn. I wasn't at all sure how our edges were supposed to fit together in the complicated puzzle of this pack-that-might-have-been.

Right now, I was desperately glad for his chapped lips sliding over mine, and his heavy-muscled arm pulling me against him almost painfully hard. As far as I was concerned, *not thinking* was the name of the game—for tonight, at least. I hadn't been exaggerating earlier. The other two would have spent a sleepless night treading and retreading the same limited set of facts in hopes of feeling more in control of events, and I would have spent a sleepless night watching them do it.

We'd have more answers tomorrow, even if they weren't answers we liked. Tonight, comfort and oblivion sounded like much more appealing options.

If nothing else, this was shaping up to be a much more civilized exit from life than the cave in Romania… so far, at least.

Jax let me up for air, and I took the chance to lean across his broad chest and catch Leo in a kiss. Her normally silky lips were chapped as well—the victim of hours of unconsciousness and the dry, recycled atmosphere in the airplane cabin. After a few moments, she pulled away and met my gaze with dark, dilated eyes.

"I want him to knot me," she said. "On a scale of one to ten, how crazy is that?"

I considered it for a moment. "It's a risk—but only if Irina lied. Though there could be hidden cameras or microphones for surveillance, I suppose."

Jax was looking between us like we were *both* crazy, which at least meant he'd stopped obsessing about Irina and Nikolayev for the moment. "If they came for us, we'd be totally vulnerable."

A stubborn gleam entered Leo's hazel eyes. "It'd be worth it to see the shock on their faces. If they hate us so damned much, they can get an eyeful of exactly what offends their fragile beta sensibilities. Fuck them all."

Maybe it was an odd thing for me to be proud about, but in that moment, I was proud of my freshly liberated *odama*. Jax let out a sharp breath and pressed his forehead against her temple for a long moment.

"Kam?" he asked. "Are you all right with this? What do you need from us?"

I tucked a strand of Leo's wild hair behind her ear. "Just let me kiss you both. That's all I want tonight."

It was the simple truth. Maybe it was the fact that I finally knew what lay on the other side of my body's capricious sexual arousal. Or maybe it was that I now knew exactly how much work was involved in getting to climax, given my body's particular... *limitations*. Whatever the case, it felt easier now to simply dwell in a low level of arousal and appreciate the feeling on its own merits. It was reminiscent of the way Leo and I used to share gentle intimacy, before this pack of alphas had come into our lives. Only, it was *more* somehow.

I could be part of this without needing to perform. My presence, accepted and desired by both of my bedmates, was enough.

Leo kissed me again, and then broke away to kiss Jax. He made a low noise and tangled his hand in her hair, taking control of her mouth while she took control of the fastenings of his trousers. I settled back to watch for a bit, breathing in the scent of aroused alpha while missing Leo's honey and orange blossom perfume—still masked beneath the pheromone suppressors Beckett had acquired for her.

She broke away with a gasp, whispering, "I love you both."

"We love you, too," I answered without hesitation.

God, how I loved her. Fiery and sweet, determined to make our fucked-up world bend to her will—even if that meant the petty defiance of taking a knot from our alpha lover in a Committee cell on the eve of our ultimate fate.

I wanted to live in the world she envisioned, where we could mate a pack of noble, adoring alphas and live together in a giant house with a cozy nest, our pups running and playing in the hallways, shrieking with happiness.

"Love you," Jax echoed quietly. "I'm sorry things couldn't be different."

"We made a difference," Leo said fiercely. "We might not have won the war, but we *did* make a difference. And we'll keep trying to make a difference until we can't anymore."

She untangled from us, but only long enough to slip off the simple sweater and leggings she'd been wearing when Nikolayev's men had taken us. Her underwear followed, exposing her petite, softly curved frame to our appreciative gazes.

Jax made a low noise, deep in his chest— and it was clear that a few days spent in Leo's heat nest had trained my body to respond to that noise. Something inside me grew soft and pliant, uncoiling from its usual tense knot.

Leo didn't waste time on foreplay. She freed Jax's cock and straddled him, sinking down on his length. He growled, the sound mellowing a moment later to a rumbling alpha purr. A whimper of pleasure escaped her in response.

"So gorgeous," Jax said. "The both of you. Kam… lose the shirt, please. I want to see more of you."

I unbuttoned the offending article of clothing in a pleasantly drugged haze, slipping out of it and pulling my white undershirt over my head as well.

"Better," Jax said, and tangled his fingers in my hair, tugging until it drew a gasp from me.

Jax had apparently been paying attention before. *Fuck.*

I melted into the pressure, but instead of dragging me to his mouth, he presented me for Leo to kiss. She attacked my lips with a ferocity I'd never felt from her before. Her fingers came up to grip my jaw, holding me where she wanted me, and I was lost.

Leo rode Jax hard, his alpha strength meeting her thrust for thrust as they passed me back and forth between them. I stopped thinking and simply *felt*, letting everything else go. Committee guards could have stormed the cell, and I still wouldn't have pulled away from the lips and teeth marking and sucking at my mouth, my jaw, my neck.

Jax nipped his way down the left side of my throat, his breath coming harsh. Leo's rhythmic, breathy cries rose in pitch as she careened toward her release, dragging Jax with her. With a final rough gasp, her muscles went rigid, and she jerked through her climax.

Jax groaned and spasmed as well. His teeth clamped over the juncture of my neck and shoulder—right over my mating gland. I cried out in a shocked combination of pleasure and pain as the skin broke, my blood and his saliva mixing. My entire body shook, gooseflesh erupting all over. My heart felt like it might explode, it was racing so fast.

The three of us remained suspended in that tableau for what seemed like a lifetime but was probably only seconds. Then Leo collapsed against Jax's chest, panting. I could feel the humid warmth of Jax's breath against my neck. He pulled back slowly, with the air of someone who'd just come back to himself and realized what he'd done.

The skin over my mating gland throbbed as the cooler air hit it. Blood beaded on Jax's lips.

"Oh fuck," he said. "*Fuck.* Kam, I'm sorry. I didn't mean—"

Dazed and knot-drunk, Leo came back to herself enough to peer at me with growing shock. I opened my mouth to say… something. Nothing came out.

"I didn't mean to…" Jax tried again. He trailed off and scrubbed at his mouth with the back of his hand. "I'm *so* sorry. I saw the scar where they took your gland. I didn't mean to bring back bad associations."

"Kam's left-glanded," Leo whispered, still watching me with wide eyes.

Jax blinked. "You're—"

I lifted a hand to the throbbing flesh. My fingers felt numb.

"Left-glanded," I repeated slowly. "They didn't get my mating gland because it's on my left shoulder, not my right. That's rare—they didn't bother to check first."

A look of blank shock washed over Jax's features. His gaze dropped to my hand covering the bite mark.

I let out a little laugh. It sounded wrong—not like a laugh at all. "Don't worry. It's as broken as the rest of me. It doesn't work anymore." I swayed a bit. "I feel strange."

"*Odama.* Come here," Leo said. She sounded like she was on the verge of tears.

I half-fell into their arms.

"Kameron," Jax said against my temple, holding me against him. "I would mate you both without a second thought. "But not like this—never like this, without asking you first."

"Don't feel too bad," I managed in a faint tone. "The joke's on you. I might be a pure-bred, but at this point, my dowry is an embarrassment."

Leo's arm tightened around me, pressing me closer between them. "Downright nonexistent," she agreed. "So's mine, by the way. You should have warned me I was supposed to have a dowry, Mr. Purebred. Is that seriously a thing?"

Jax had gone very still, as though he couldn't believe we were joking about it.

"I wouldn't worry about it," I told her. "Probably a bit moot under the circumstances." I shifted in their arms, a bit uncomfortably. "Though, if you could get your mouth back on that and stop the bleeding, it would be much appreciated, alpha."

Jax hesitated, but after a moment he scooted me a bit farther up his body and lowered his lips to my shoulder, pressing an achingly soft kiss there before covering the bite wound and rasping his tongue across the ragged skin. I closed my eyes against the fresh flood of full-body tingles—mated in the eyes of a legal system that no longer existed... and in none of the ways that actually mattered. *Oh, the irony.*

SIXTEEN

Leo

JAX AND I held Kam between us. Shock at what had just happened swirled with the pleasure pulsing through my core from the knot tying us together.

I didn't think Kam was angry or even upset at Jax's lapse of control. Of our three alphas, I would have pegged Jax as by far the least likely to slip like that—but I'd also been painfully aware that he was struggling emotionally, reeling from both the loss of his pack and our capture, followed by Irina's revelation. Of course, he'd had no way of knowing that the ugly scar on Kam's right shoulder hadn't succeeded in its aim of destroying his mating gland. In the absence of the swelling and redness that came with an omega's heat cycle, his left shoulder just looked like any other normal stretch of skin.

Rather than talk the situation to death, we just clung. Jax's woodsy scent tickled my nostrils, and his big hands wrapped around us both, holding tight. Eventually, the lingering pleasure eased, my body relaxing its grip and allowing Jax's knot to go down. I eased off him, kissing his lips and Kam's temple.

"Stay here," I told them. "I want to clean up a bit, and then I'll be right back."

Jax nodded. Kam made a half-aware, sleepy noise.

The facilities were basic—a sink and a toilet—but still miles better than the terrorist cave. There was toilet paper available, along with disposable hand towels, so I took care of business and managed a quick wash. Wetting a couple of the paper towels with warm water, I returned and handed one to Jax. The other, I used to dab at the bite mark on Kam's shoulder. It was inflamed but no longer bleeding… alpha saliva having done its job to begin the healing process.

Everything I knew about mating, I knew from Kam. Just as the removal of Irina's mating gland would have disrupted her pregnancy, in the absence of the rest of Kam's reproductive system, his mating gland would no longer function properly. There would be no genetic pairing, no psychic bond.

At least, that was the theory.

"Any side effects, either of you?" I asked cautiously.

Kam shook his head wordlessly, not lifting it from Jax's chest. Jax had finished cleaning himself up and refastened his pants one-handed, still holding Kam against his side.

"No," he said softly. "I don't feel anything."

I retrieved my clothing from the floor and pulled it on except for my bra, turning my panties inside out in the absence of clean underwear. I took a certain vicious satisfaction in the knowledge that this room would reek of sex when our captors arrived in the morning. But I was not, in fact, in any hurry to have the guards burst in on us while I was naked.

After throwing the used paper towels away, I rejoined the pair on the bed and pulled the blanket up to cover all three of us. The mattress was honestly too small for this, but I couldn't imagine sleeping anywhere else.

———◆———

The presence of warm bodies next to me combined with my post-orgasmic haze meant that I slept better than I might have expected. Kam was subdued when we finally awoke. Jax was already back to restless frustration, up before us and pacing the room.

"All right?" I asked Kam, stretching cautiously.

"Sore shoulder," he said. "That's all."

I wondered if he would have preferred the mating to take root, even though it had been unplanned. Somehow, it seemed like a really bad idea to ask.

Breakfast arrived—some kind of porridge with paper cartons of orange juice. Scarcely had we finished it when the lock clanked and the door swung open again. Two armed guards entered, weapons raised and pointed at Jax, who rose slowly from his chair.

The fine hair on the back of my neck prickled as a third figure entered.

Kostya Nikolayev looked like a man exercising iron control to hide the fact that he was coming apart at the seams. Frustrated energy crackled around him, and his steel-gray eyes snapped fire. But even in the wilderness of southern Cuba, his charcoal two-piece suit was impeccable.

"Leona McCready," he said, in his rich Russian accent. "Come with me. We must speak now."

Jax tensed, and I had the horrible feeling he was doing the mental math to decide if he could lunge forward and break Nikolayev's neck before falling over dead beneath a hail of gunfire from the guards. My own heart pounded uncontrollably, but I threw up a hand toward him, palm out, and said, "Jax. *Don't.*"

This was what I'd asked for, after all. I didn't want to have to worry about Jax erupting into violence while I was trying to decipher the finer details of this situation. I also didn't want Kam present, where he might be used against me. Of course, I was deluding myself—he and Jax could be used against me just as easily while they were trapped in this cell. It still made me feel better not to have them directly under Nikolayev's angry gaze, though.

"Don't," I repeated. "It's all right. I'll be back in a bit... or possibly, I won't be. Either way, I love you both. Never forget that."

Jax looked like he was holding onto his control like a thread. Kam had the expression of someone who knew exactly what it was like to watch a loved one walk out of a room for the last time. I wrenched my eyes away from them and turned to the Committee chairman.

"Lead on, then," I said.

The guards escorted me out. A moment later, the door to the cell snicked shut and locked behind me, cutting me off from my fracturing alpha and my sad-eyed *odama*. The security door in the hallway opened for us, and then it too, slammed closed behind us. Nikolayev led the way deeper into the building, the two armed guards flanking me in clear threat.

We ended up in a conference room. It wasn't large, but it was oddly normal looking—like any such room you might find inside an average office building. Nikolayev gestured me curtly to a seat and dismissed the guards, who left without a word.

"Not worried I'll try to shiv you with the plastic spoon from breakfast?" I asked, fighting the damned omega compulsion to bare my throat to this overpowering terror of a man.

"I have neither the time nor the patience for banter," Nikolayev said. "No more than I have time for your alpha's dramatics. Give me all the information you have on Rhys Beckett's disappearance."

"To what end?" I asked. "You'll forgive me if I'm not in a hurry to answer, when you want to see him dead as much or more than Sloane does."

It was a risky opening gambit, and indeed, Nikolayev's eyes flared with murder for a split second before he hid the expression behind a granite mask. Nevertheless, I needed to understand what was happening here before I started handing out information that might come back to bite the entire alphomic underground in the ass.

"I intend to retrieve Beckett from Sloane's custody," Nikolayev said, biting the words off. "By force, if necessary."

"Okay," I replied. "Let's dig into that a bit further, please. Why should I consider it preferable for Beckett to be in your custody rather than Sloane's? What are you offering that would make it a good deal for me? Because it sounds an awful lot like exchanging the frying pan for the fire."

Nikolayev stared at me. It felt like he was staring *through* me. I valiantly tried to hide the shudder that wanted to break free.

"You know better than that, *Ambassador McCready*." His voice lowered to a lethal purr, and he placed heavy irony on the title. "Or have you so quickly forgotten our mutually beneficial exchange in Montreal?"

His presence felt like a physical pressure in the atmosphere, weighing down my shoulders—trying to make me bend beneath it. It was all I could do to hold his gaze, unblinking.

"Are you implying the possibility of concessions in exchange for getting what you want?" I asked. "Because I feel I must point out that when you had dealings with me before in Montreal, you thought I was a beta."

He raised an eyebrow—though I got the impression he was working hard to convey that level of insouciance. "Did I indeed? You are aware of my reputation, are you not?"

That stopped me in my mental tracks.

They say he can sniff out an omega at twenty paces, even with pheromone suppressors.

Had he known, even back then? That was what he was implying, and not very subtly. It might be the truth, or it might be a lie. But if it was true, it meant that Nikolayev was not, in fact, hell-bent on mindlessly catching and killing every hidden omega in existence. Which made him more strategic than I'd given him credit for. And, if possible, even more dangerous.

"Do you want Beckett dead?" I asked bluntly, focusing every omega sense I had on his body language—searching for deception.

"No," he replied blandly.

"Do you want him alive so you can torture the same information out of him that Sloane's after?" I pressed.

"I don't need his information," Nikolayev ground out. "I only need to ensure Sloane doesn't get it."

Every instinct I possessed screamed that I shouldn't be able to get under Kostya Nikolayev's skin this easily. I shouldn't be able to interrogate him like this. I was a known omega fugitive—his prisoner. This was wrong, wrong, *wrong*... but I couldn't see the lie. I couldn't see the shape of the gap where the puzzle pieces were missing.

"I require that you exercise whatever persuasion is necessary to tame your angry alpha so I can use him in the retrieval mission," he said. "Do you have an active mate-bond with the two alphas Sloane captured to use as leverage?"

"*What*? Why?" I demanded, completely derailed yet again.

"*Answer the question.*"

It was a bark worthy of an alpha, and my spine snapped straight beneath it. "No!" I gasped, before clawing back a shred of control. "No, we're not mated."

He made a hissing noise that brought to mind the reptile I'd accused him of being.

"What does that have to do with any of this?" I asked.

"Tactical advantage," he snapped.

Had he wanted to use the psychic connection between mated pack members as some sort of... *location tracking*? Did it even work that way?

It was a gamble, but I was about to concede on the basis that being physically reunited with Beckett and the others was better than being separated. Together we were stronger, surely. I pushed my reservations aside.

"I'll get Jax on board, but only with conditions. You also retrieve the two alphas Sloane is holding as leverage against Beckett."

Nikolayev sneered at me. "I'm hardly likely to leave Sloane with that kind of *leverage*, as you put it."

Making sure that Sloane didn't keep Flynn and Alex *could* mean rescuing them along with Beckett. It could also mean killing them as a means of removing them from the chessboard.

"And Irina leads the rescue mission," I went on, banking on the omega being more inclined to retrieve her former mate than put a bullet in her head. *Please, let that be a reasonable assumption on my part.*

"Relying on sentiment?" Nikolayev mocked, confirming that he knew very well of the connection between his soldier and one of Sloane's prisoners. "Very well. I concede to your demands. Now tell me what you know."

Hoping I wasn't making a horrible mistake with all of this, I recounted the events surrounding Beckett's disappearance, as I knew them.

When I was done, he nodded. "You will be returned to your cell now. You have thirty minutes to convince your guard dog to do as he's told."

"Wait," I said quickly, before he could turn around and stalk out. "Irina. You know very well who and what she is. Why is she working for you? Why isn't she dead?"

"Only a fool wastes a valuable asset," he replied, his mind clearly focused on organizing the retrieval mission. He paused, pinning me with those piercing gray eyes again before adding, "And you should know that Enoch Sloane is most *definitely* a fool of the first order."

With that, he did leave, and was replaced immediately by the two guards. They marched me back to my cell—and the alpha I was about to try and convince to join a paramilitary operation under the command of a man we all hated.

SEVENTEEN

Jax

MY RELIEF AT Leona's safe return did nothing to make me like what I was hearing any better.

"And the bastard wants me to come along on this so-called 'retrieval mission' *because*…?" I asked.

Leona sighed. "To begin with, he apparently thought we were all mated. I think he wanted to use the bond as some sort of tracking aid, or… something. Now that he knows we're not, I'm pretty sure he wants you there so Alex, Flynn, and Beckett won't fight back against his people while they're trying to extract them."

"I'm supposed to be the fucking Judas goat?" I said. "No, thank you."

Kam had been watching the exchange. At that, he spoke up. "Leo. You agreed to this. What are you seeing here that we're not?"

"Or did he force you to agree by threatening us if you didn't?" I added, since that seemed like an obvious possibility.

"Oddly enough, he didn't," she replied. "Here's the way I'm looking at it. If we're all together, we have a slightly better chance than if we're separated. And while I don't claim to know what game Nikolayev is playing, I *absolutely* know what game Sloane's playing. If Sloane gets the name of Beckett's mate, it sounds like that's going to be a disaster for everyone."

"And if Nikolayev gets it instead?" I asked.

She pulled out a chair and sat down. "I'm not sure. Sloane wants to burn down the world and rebuild it in his own image. I get the impression Nikolayev would prefer there to still be a functioning global society at the end of the day, because he knows that being the king of a smoldering wasteland isn't much of an accomplishment."

Kam, who'd been sitting on the bed, nodded thoughtfully. His hand lifted to rub absently at his left shoulder, where I'd bitten him. I wasn't sure he was even aware he was doing it.

"The Committee only exists as long as it has an enemy to rally people against," he said slowly. "As long as there's a credible threat of alphomic rebellion bubbling beneath the surface, Nikolayev has a job, not to mention an infrastructure funneling money and influence in his direction. But if alphas and omegas no longer pose any sort of threat in the minds of his followers..." He trailed off and shrugged.

"He's under pressure." Leona met my eyes frankly. "I don't know if the threat of losing his position would be enough to account for it, but I'll stake my life that he's fraying at the edges right now. It makes me wonder if there's more to Beckett and his secrets than we know about."

"So you want to try and get the others into the custody of the slightly less insane Committee chairman," I said. "What if you're wrong about this, and the fact that Nikolayev isn't as much of a nutjob as Sloane means that he's actually *more* dangerous?"

"It's possible," she said. "Here's the thing, though. Nothing's stopping Nikolayev from having Kam and me hauled out of this cell under threat of immediate death if you don't do exactly what he tells you to. I'm wondering why he didn't lead with that, personally."

My lips twisted, old bitterness getting the best of me. "Easy. A willing slave is always better than an unwilling one."

"There's also Irina," Kam said. "There was nothing stopping him from sending her to the executioner after she was arrested and tried. But he didn't."

I could feel my blood pressure spike at the mention of Alex's traitorous mate. "Maybe that says more about her than it does about him," I bit out.

"No," Leo said flatly. "It *really* doesn't."

"She wasn't the one with the power," Kam said. "Unless she had some kind of information valuable enough to use as blackmail against Nikolayev, he had all the leverage, and she had none."

"Even if she did have something to use against him," Leo added, "killing the blackmailer usually solves those kinds of problems. Also, if she were being kept alive because she's got dirt on Nikolayev, it would make a lot more sense to pay her off and hide her away someplace safe and obscure, rather than putting her in a position of power within a private paramilitary force."

My instincts clamored against collaborating with these assholes who were holding us prisoner, but Leona had a point that if Nikolayev decided to force my hand, he had two very good ways to do so.

"You both want me to do this?" I asked.

They exchanged one of those looks that contained an entire wordless conversation.

Leo was the one to answer. "We know the others are in a horrific situation right now — probably undergoing torture. No matter how strong Beckett is, you know he loves the three of you like his own pups. He won't last forever before he breaks."

The words were like a knife in the gut, twisting and tearing. I had to physically stop myself from hunching over beneath their force.

"If they're here with us, it might end up being better and it might end up being worse," Leo said softly. "But at least we'll be together, and we can go from there."

There was a painful pause.

"All right," I managed eventually, well aware that I was a nerve-damaged emotional wreck who probably had no business getting within ten miles of a covert ops mission.

Leo nodded. "I insisted Irina be the one to command the mission. With luck, that will ensure Flynn and Alex get out alive, along with Beckett. Nikolayev won't let Sloane keep them, but I'm not entirely convinced he cares all that much how they're taken off the board."

"Either we'll all get out or none of us will," I vowed, aware that might not have sounded terribly reassuring.

"We know," Kam said. "Go and bring them back to us, okay?"

<hr>

Nikolayev didn't keep us in suspense long. Irina arrived roughly half an hour after Leona had been returned to our cell.

"Are we good, then?" she asked, her hand resting not-so-casually on the grip of her sidearm.

"Yeah," I said, my hands clenching into fists beneath the cover of the table. "Fucking *stellar*."

She cocked an eyebrow at me. "Glad to hear it. Say goodbye to your omegas and shift your ass, in that case. The clock's ticking."

The idea of leaving Leona and Kameron defenseless in Nikolayev's custody went against every alpha instinct I possessed. All at once, I wanted to grab Irina by the shoulders and shake her until her teeth rattled and answers fell out. I swallowed the impulse down—bitter and acidic in my throat.

Leo touched my shoulder. "Try to get them back for us, Jax. We'll be here waiting."

I reached out and clasped my hand around the back of her neck, pulling her in for a fierce kiss. She kissed back with equal fierceness, easing away with a final sharp nip to my lower lip. I'd be feeling the tingle for hours.

Kam had been hanging back, his arms crossed defensively in front of him. "You should be aware that it's considered awfully bad form to get yourself killed in order to wiggle out of an accidental mating," he said in a mild tone.

I pushed away from the table and rose, crossing to him and cupping his face in my hands. The left one shook, damaged nerves fighting against my brain's control.

"Wouldn't dream of it, Ginger Tea," I told him, borrowing Flynn's nickname. I pressed a chaste kiss to his forehead. Pulling back, I handed him off to Leo, who wrapped an arm around his shoulders. "Try not to scandalize the beta bigots too much while I'm gone, okay?"

"*Hmph.* Where's the fun in that?" Leo asked, playing at bravado. "Go on, now—but hurry back. We'll miss you."

I closed my eyes, took a slow breath, then nodded and turned away to follow Irina out of the cell.

———◆———

"Give me a rundown of your physical limitations," Irina said as we marched down the endless corridors that seemed to define this place. "Something fucked you up bad. What was it, and how serious is the damage?"

"Intravenous dose of an experimental VX nerve agent variant," I replied, aware that since I was doing this, I would have to play by the rules set for me by my traitorous shit of a temporary commanding officer. "I have headaches and intermittent muscle weakness on the left side."

"How's your head right now?" she asked, as though she didn't actually give a fuck.

"Pounding like a drum," I informed her in the same tone.

She shot me a sidelong glance. "Can you see straight enough to hit a target?"

My lip curled. "Ask the grunts you sent to take us down in New York."

"The fact that they're all still alive isn't exactly a ringing endorsement," she said tartly.

"Wasn't aiming for them," I lied. "I was aiming for the goddamn floodlights they were using to blind us."

"Sure you were," she replied, in a tone that said she was humoring me. "Fine — as long as you're clear on which direction to point the end that goes *boom*."

"Don't fucking tempt me," I muttered, and stopped abruptly. The guards behind us gripped their weapons warily, but Irina halted and turned to face me.

"What is it?" she asked.

I stared down at her tiny frame. "You want this mission to go smoothly? Do *not* reveal yourself to Alex until after we're safely out. Let's just say, she isn't going to take any of this well."

Irina let out an indelicate snort and started walking again. "You think? Yes, your tactical advice is noted. Thank you *so* much."

I clenched my jaw against the throbbing pain in my skull and started after her. We ended up in a quartermaster's supply room, where I was kitted out in state-of-the-art black tactical gear.

"Weapons?" I asked.

"Sure," she said. "When we're ready to go in, and I can be relatively certain you'll have other things to worry about besides putting a slug in me or one of my men."

The next stop on the itinerary was the briefing. Apparently, Nikolayev was in a big hurry when it came to implementing his plan, because he certainly wasn't waiting around on things. I thought back to what Leona had said earlier.

I'll stake my life that he's fraying at the edges right now.

According to the briefing, Beckett and the others were being held at a secure facility near the Alabama coast—a six hundred mile flight that we would be making in a convoy of three Black Hawk helicopters, each one outfitted with an ERFS long-range fuel system. Since the choppers would be broadcasting legitimate Committee identification codes, the plan was to land inside the compound and swarm the facility's security forces, using the element of surprise to power our way in, secure the three targets, and get out the same way before back-up could arrive.

It was the kind of brute-force attack that appealed to me, both for its simplicity and for the opportunity it was likely to provide to bash some heads. It wasn't, however, the kind of plan I would have pictured Nikolayev coming up with. Of course, his normal job involved bullying politicians and arranging firing squads. Nothing I'd ever heard about him mentioned anything about a military background. He probably had other people to strategize helicopter raids for him.

There were schematics showing a basic layout of the target facility—possibly gleaned from satellite intel—but they were light on detail. In many ways, we would be going in blind—and apparently in broad daylight as well.

Irina's eyes landed on me heavily. "At no time during our mission will anyone here identify yourselves to the three targets as being associated with either the Committee or Chairman Nikolayev. Is that clear?"

"Crystal," I said, as the others in the room muttered acknowledgement. And wasn't *that* going to make the conversation I had with Alex and Flynn afterward a real treat? Assuming we survived long enough to have it, of course.

Hi, guys — sorry I failed to mention that I helped drag you out of Sloane's hands so I could dump you into Nikolayev's, instead… because apparently I'm working for the Euro-Soviet Committee now. Leona asked me to do it, you see — and, well, it seemed like a good idea at the time.

On second thought, maybe I should leave the explanations to her and Kam, assuming the six of us weren't chained up in separate dungeons by that point. Christ, what a goddamned mess.

After a few more minutes of tactical briefing, Irina ran her cool gray gaze over the assemblage. "That's it, soldiers. Let's go steal some prisoners. Departure is scheduled in fifteen minutes."

EIGHTEEN

Jax

EACH CHOPPER had a pilot, a copilot, two crew chiefs, six soldiers, and two stretchers aboard. As soon as I was strapped in, Irina handed me a bottle of water and two pills.

"Aspirin," she said. "For your head."

"Thanks." I palmed the pills rather than swallowing them, since I had no way of knowing what the hell they actually were. When I was sure no one was looking, I stuck them in a convenient pocket in my tactical vest. Maybe there was no obvious reason why she'd want me incapacitated before the mission, but I wasn't about to take a chance she might slip me something to make me more compliant or biddable.

The seal on the plastic bottle cap was intact, so I did at least drink the water.

It had been a while since I'd flown any appreciable distance in a helicopter. Ignoring the pounding pain in my skull, I donned my headset and tested the push-to-talk button on the cord, familiarizing myself with the unit.

Within minutes, the engine roared to life. The rotor spun up, and we were off. This would be a twelve hundred mile round trip, mostly over water, with enough fuel for thirteen hundred eighty miles on a good day. There wasn't a huge margin for error, especially if someone in Sloane's compound knocked a few brain cells together and managed to shoot out one of the chopper's external fuel tanks.

It was a calculated risk, since a refueling stop was impractical. Get in, get out, get back to Cuba. That was the long and the short of the mission.

The three-and-a-half hour flight dragged, but the closer we got to our destination, the more my damned alpha instincts took over. My pack was in trouble, and I was coming to get them out. The rightness of that part of things threatened to overwhelm the very real fact that I was following the orders of *Kostya fucking Nikolayev*, and I'd basically just sold my soul to the Committee on the basis of Leona McCready's hunch.

Get them out safe, and worry about the rest of it later, I told myself firmly. It wasn't as though I could change my mind now, with the Alabama coastline a brown and green smear in front of us.

Irina was strapped in directly across from me. Her gray eyes had barely left me during the long flight, but she'd wisely refrained from trying to make conversation over the headset. I got the impression that she was a focused and no-nonsense commander in the field—not surprising, given what I'd known of her from the time before the mess with Alex.

Now, she pulled out a semi-automatic pistol and checked the clip before handing it across to me. It was a SIG P210, stamped with the Swiss army designation in the serial number. I checked the safety and pulled back the slide, chambering a round before stowing the gun into my shoulder holster, cocked and locked. Irina passed over four extra magazines. Forty rounds. I supposed if I ended up needing more than that, it would mean we had bigger worries to contend with.

I offered her a wary nod of acknowledgement.

We were approaching land. In the cockpit, the pilot hailed someone, speaking in a bland UFNA Midwest accent at odds with the Eastern European drawl I'd heard in my headset earlier.

I supposed that if you were going to try and infiltrate a Committee facility by air, actually being part of the Committee was a big help. The mic from the cockpit cut out. Presumably, the pilot and whoever he was talking to had started exchanging sensitive security codes.

If clearance wasn't granted, we'd bluster our way in regardless. Sloane's compound was unlikely to have robust ground-to-air defenses... *supposedly*. It was a prison facility, not a military installation. Besides, the list of organizations that would dare attack the Committee openly like this was, shall we say, somewhat limited.

Long minutes passed before the mic crackled into life again.

"Landing clearance granted," the pilot said in his native accent. "ETA in eighteen minutes."

"Prep for action, boys," Irina said crisply. "We only get one shot at this."

———◆———

Sloane's compound screamed 'prison' in a way that Nikolayev's property in Cuba didn't. It was likely that it had, in fact, been a federal or state correctional facility in its former life. Chain link fencing and razor wire surrounded the stark rectangular concrete building, while guard towers dotted the perimeter.

Those towers would be the first order of business, but they weren't my problem. I was part of the tactical group tasked with retrieving Flynn and Alex. Meanwhile, Irina would be leading the group going after Beckett, on the assumption that he was likely being held in high-security solitary confinement.

All of Nikolayev's forces would be wearing balaclavas to hide their faces—all except me. My Judas goat role relied on letting my packmates see me and be reassured enough to let a bunch of armed troops drag them onto a helicopter.

The political fallout of our smash-and-grab operation was outside of my purview, and I wasn't sure I really gave a shit about it anyway. I wondered, though, if Nikolayev would plead complete innocence when Sloane came screaming to him afterward, blaming the breach on lax security in Sloane's own operation and using any security footage of my face as supporting evidence of an alphomic operation, perhaps by the underground Sloane was so set on dismantling.

Again—not my problem. I'd have plenty of fallout of my own to deal with, once the others realized what I'd done.

The chopper settled onto the helipad on the building's roof. Around us, the other two would have done the same, landing in a triangular nose-to-tail configuration that gave the door-mounted machine guns on the outer sides complete three hundred and sixty degree access to our surroundings.

We waited—unstrapped from our seatbelts and ready to move fast when the order came.

Within minutes the roof access door opened, and a delegation in blue uniforms approached. I had a perfect view through the open side door of the helicopter as the machine guns opened fire and mowed them down before turning their collective firepower on the guard turrets.

Glass shattered, ensuring that the chaos inside the towers would delay any return fire, on the off chance that any of the guards inside had survived. We poured out of the choppers, guns drawn. Those of us assigned to the two retrieval teams made straight for the roof entrance, while the remaining troops dug in around the helicopters, ready to protect our only transportation out of here.

The door was locked—proof that the people who'd come out to meet us weren't complete idiots, at least. Irina stuck a directed explosive charge over the mechanism, and we fell back as it deployed with a dull *crump*. The door swung open, the metal warped and glowing red where the lock had been blown out. Around us, klaxons began to wail.

We swarmed inside. Those in the lead shot down the handful of guards rushing up the stairwell to meet us. I hopped over the slumped bodies as we hurried downward into the guts of the building, cursing the weakness on my left side as my leg threatened to waver beneath the extra strain.

Those damned klaxons weren't doing a thing for my aching head, either.

The helipad stairwell led down to the admin wing, as we'd anticipated. Security wasn't as tight here as it would be in the prisoner areas, and we only had to blow one more door to gain access to the main administration area. Terrified desk jockeys huddled inside offices with inadequate wooden doors—easy to kick down.

"Who in here knows where the high-value prisoners are being kept?" my team leader—a beta male named Kowalczyk—bellowed in a passable UFNA accent. "Point them out or we mow down everyone in this room!"

Several tentative fingers pointed toward a harried looking man in a tan suit, whose face paled when he realized his colleagues had just given him up for slaughter like a Christmas turkey.

"The rest of you lie face down on the ground!" Kowalczyk ordered, while two other soldiers grabbed the guy in the suit. One of them jammed a gun in his ribs, and a high-pitched whimper of fear escaped him.

"Out," the trooper with the gun ordered, managing a less convincing attempt at a local accent.

We left the other admin workers cowering on the ground, waiting until we were back outside before Kowalczyk grabbed the man's jaw in one meaty hand and said, "Lead us to the omega named Rhys Beckett and the alphas designated Alex and Flynn, or I shoot out both your kneecaps."

The man was practically gibbering in fear. "B-b-but you won't be able to get to them! The security—"

"Is our concern," Kowalczyk cut in. "Your concern is the unbearable pain and permanent disability that will result if you provoke me into shooting you. I can always find another office drudge to tell me what I want to know."

I had to give it to the man... he had 'dead-eyed and terrifying' down to an art form. Not normally a compliment, true—but it was useful under the circumstances. My sensitive alpha nose detected the smell of urine a couple of seconds before the dark stain appeared on the office guy's trousers. *Classy.*

Kowalczyk released the man's jaw with a look of disgust.

"I c-can take you, but I don't have keys for the checkpoints," the guy stammered.

"We don't need keys," Kowalczyk said, and stepped back, gesturing with his gun. *"Move."*

One of the soldiers shoved him, and the man stumbled forward.

"Th-this way," he said, gesturing toward a set of double doors.

Both teams made their way into the prisoner wing at the guy's direction. Irina was staying inconspicuous, I couldn't help noticing. It made sense. Even if she could pull off the accent, the presence of a small woman in a paramilitary operation was too memorable. From what I understood during the briefing, they wanted any surviving witnesses to remember only a bunch of masked, black-clad goons with guns... except for me, with my face bare for the world to see.

Judas goat and sacrificial lamb all rolled up in one neat package, I thought. *Just tie a fuckin' bell to my neck next time.*

We ran into guards in twos and threes, re-inforcing the idea that places like this were geared toward preventing the people inside from getting out, not preventing people outside from getting in. At least, not if those people were armed, trained, and possessed explosives.

The first few prison guards fell before they could even get a shot off. When we had to stop and blow the lock on yet another security door, it gave the guards inside enough time to set up an ambush. Bullets flew as soon as the door swung open. We were hugging the walls in anticipation of such an attack, but one of Niko-layev's men went down with half of his neck blown away.

Irina pulled a flash-bang grenade from her belt and tossed it through the door. I turned away and covered my ears. After the blinding light stopped spearing through my tightly closed eyelids, I stormed into the newly opened section with the others and gunned down two guards who were struggling to re-gain their feet.

The others took care of the rest. Kow-alczyk confronted the admin guy, who was clutching at his right ear, tears streaking down his bloodless face.

"I can't hear!" he said, too loudly. *"I've gone deaf!"*

Kowalczyk stared him down, muttering, *"Fuck's sake."* He lowered the muzzle of his gun meaningfully toward the man's knees.

"It's th-this way," office guy said, pointing with the hand that wasn't still cradling his ear. "S-sorry. Left at the next junction! That's the high security wing!"

We waded through the carnage in the corridor, toward the next T-junction. Four more of Sloane's guards shuffled off this mortal coil beneath a hail of our gunfire, and eventually we reached a door marked *MAXIMUM SECURITY* in bold, blocky lettering.

Thankfully, the door itself was no different to any of the others we'd blown open. The corridor beyond was oddly deserted. The lack of an active defense prickled the hair on the back of my neck. Cameras whirred, their red eyes watching us from the ceiling.

"The omega will be in interrogation room one," office guy babbled. "The alphas will be in interrogation room t-two! Now please let me go, *please*! I did what you asked!"

Kowalczyk nodded to the man's guards. The one who'd held a gun on him lifted it and shot him through the head without comment. Office guy slumped to the floor, twitching.

Irina exchanged a glance with Kowalczyk and made the hand signal for 'split up.' The two teams would peel off to retrieve our separate targets, and then try to get the hell out before anyone in the facility managed to get outside backup involved.

Each team had started out with six soldiers. Ours was down to five, and one of Irina's was bleeding from the shoulder. It didn't matter—we were close enough to Beckett and my packmates that I could practically smell them. The pounding agony in my skull had faded to something distant and unimportant. The weakness in my ravaged body wouldn't slow me down because I wouldn't let it. My senses thrummed, wondering where the trap was.

Interrogation Room One was at the end of the corridor. It killed me inside not to hang back and watch as Irina and her team prepared to force their way in, but that wasn't my part of the mission. Interrogation Room Two was around the corner. My heart pounded, driving blood through my veins and strength to my muscles as Kowalczyk set the directed charge above the lock. The five of us pressed our backs to the wall on either side of the door.

Crump, and the door swung open a few inches, off-kilter on its hinges. Kowalczyk kicked it open and promptly went down with a cry, blood spurting from an artery in his thigh. Through the open door, I got a confused impression of a man in a guard uniform, a second man in a white lab coat cowering behind a table... and Flynn chained naked to the wall with a pair of battery leads clamped to his chest.

With a roar, I put my head down and charged the man with the gun.

NINETEEN

Flynn

MY HEAD MIGHT have been fuzzing in and out like a television with poor reception, but when one of the torturers *du jour* stepped away to answer the phone hanging on the wall by the door, I knew something was up.

Alex was either down for the count or faking unconsciousness after Goon Number Two had finished breaking the last two fingers on her left hand—I wasn't sure which. We'd both been giving these fuckers false information for the past day and a half, singing like canaries without letting anything important slip. Problem was, they weren't torturing us because they wanted us to talk. They were torturing us because they wanted *Beckett* to talk.

It didn't take a rocket scientist to guess why there were enough cameras pointed at us to film a big budget Hollywood movie. We might not have seen Beckett ourselves, but he was here. I was sure of it. When the phone call came through and the goons started acting nervous, you can bet I was listening with both ears—even if I didn't lift my head from where it lolled against my chest.

The words *'security breach'* and *'armed intruders approaching'* were sweet music to my ears. Yeah, it could have been completely unrelated to us… but I was betting it wasn't. I was betting it was Jax. I didn't claim to have a clue how he might have gathered the kind of assault force that could break into a Committee holding facility. Maybe the underground had military assets Alex and I didn't know about. Maybe Beckett was an important enough cog in the wheel to inspire them to use those assets.

Didn't matter.

What *did* matter was that I was still naked and chained to the back wall like a goddamned bull's eye target, though they'd at least stopped shocking me in favor of losing their shit over whatever was happening outside. I was about to be an eyewitness to whatever went down next—though not a very good one, since one of my eyes was already swollen shut and the other one was well on the way.

I couldn't get loose on my own. Best-case scenario, I'd get a front-row seat to someone putting bullets in these assholes. Worst case, I'd be in the line of fire as well, and end up bleeding out before I got the satisfaction of seeing them all die.

Goon Number One hung up the phone. "Take cover and be ready. Grab that one and get out of sight behind the door," he snapped to Goon Number Two, pointing at Alex's crumpled form. Then he drew his gun and positioned himself in a classic firing stance several feet back from the doorway.

The second goon dragged Alex to the wall on the far side of the door, where it would block them from view if it opened. She didn't stir as he crouched behind her and hauled her upper body against his so he could jam the muzzle of his gun against her temple. Meanwhile, the mealy-mouthed lab tech in his white coat ducked behind the table that held the voltage regulator and various other torture devices, as though he thought that was what 'taking cover' meant.

The walls were thick in this place, but I thought I could make out muffled boot steps pounding in the corridor outside. *Show time.*

The sound of a directed explosive charge was shockingly loud as it echoed off the concrete walls of the room. Smoke and dust obscured the view for a moment, but I heard the creak of tortured hinges that meant the door had given way.

Metal shrieked as it swung wider, possibly beneath the force of a kick. A man stood silhouetted in the gap for a bare second before Goon Number One squeezed off a round. The silhouette crumpled to the ground with a hoarse cry.

A second figure appeared in the gap with a roar of rage and charged, leading with his right shoulder. I caught a flash of blond hair, and I *knew*. It was Jax. I still had no clue how the fucking bastard had managed to organize this, but somehow he had.

Goon Number One fired off another wild shot, though he must have known that nothing short of a bullet through the heart or the brain was going to stop an enraged alpha mid-charge. Jax plowed into him like a rugby player and they both went down. My packmate drew back the hand that held his weapon and landed a savage blow with the butt of the pistol. The goon went limp.

Jax staggered to his feet, his blue eyes feral with rage as he took me in.

"Check your five," I rasped.

He whirled, raising his sidearm—his gaze swinging to the five o'clock position where Goon Number Two still had a gun pressed to Alex's head. Three other soldiers kitted out in black gear and balaclavas charged in, following Jax's line of sight to the pair huddled on the floor. Two of them aimed handguns at Alex and the goon, while the third covered Lab Boy, still cowering behind the table with his clipboard.

"Drop it," Jax ground out.

"Fuck off," said the goon. "You gonna shoot through her to get to me?"

"Why not?" asked one of the other men. Something about his accent sounded odd. I couldn't quite place it. "What do we care about some hyena bitch?"

A muscle in Jax's jaw twitched. I started planning ways to use the torture instruments lying conveniently on the table if anyone shot Alex. What the hell kind of mercenaries was Jax using for this operation, anyway?

"Hey, fucker," I snarled. "Try it, and see what happens."

Alex chose that moment to explode into life. She wrenched her upper body forward and drove her elbow back, twisting like a snake to get her unbroken right hand around Goon Number Two's wrist, jerking his gun hand up. The pistol went off, the bullet embedding itself in the ceiling and sending chips of concrete shrapnel raining down. A heartbeat later, the weapon was in Alex's hand and pointed at her captor's head. Another explosion of sound, and Goon Number Two's brains splattered against the wall behind him.

I gave her a quick onceover. Then I gave Jax a quick onceover, taking in the wet patch on his left thigh. "You're bleeding, asshole," I said, jerking my chin at the shiny stain.

He glanced down. "Mother *fucker*," he said, and shot the unconscious goon he'd tackled to the ground earlier. The gun swung toward Lab Boy, who was hunched against the wall now, holding his clipboard in front of his chest like he could use it to stop a bullet.

"You," Jax said. "Get him out of those chains."

Lab Boy froze for a second, his eyes as wide as dinner plates. Then he pointed at the man Alex had killed. "That guard had the keys."

"Then I expect he still does," Jax snapped. "So fucking *get them.*"

The tech scurried into motion, every gun in the room trained on him as he fumbled through Goon Number Two's pockets and came up with the keys. His already pale face whitened further as he cautiously approached me and reached for the first wrist shackle. I grinned down at him, showing teeth, and his pale eyes darted away nervously. The second wrist shackle followed the first. I stood still and docile as he crouched down to get the ankle shackles.

When I was finally free, I pulled the electrical leads off my nipples and tossed them aside. Next, I reached down and grabbed Lab Boy by the neck, spinning him to face away from me. I ignored the pain of abused muscle and bone as I got a grip on his chin with my other hand and twisted. His startled yelp cut off in a crunch of bone and cartilage. I let the body slump to the ground and stepped around it, since I hurt too fucking much to step over it if I didn't have to.

Crouching down to pick up Goon Number One's gun was agony, but damned if I was walking out of this room unarmed. I managed to regain my feet without falling over and turned a scowl on the soldier who'd threatened to shoot through Alex to get to his target.

"Are you and me gonna have a problem?" I asked.

"Stow it," Alex croaked, cutting me off. "Exit plan?"

"Choppers on the roof," Jax said. "We need to move."

He didn't ask if we could make it under our own power. Bastard knew us too well for that. One of the other soldiers knelt to check the pulse of the guy who'd been shot in the doorway and shook his head.

"Leave him," said the guy who'd called Alex a hyena. Apparently, he was a cold-hearted bastard all around, then—not that I was about to argue the call. Last thing we needed was to have to haul a corpse through a battle zone.

The others cleared the corridor and set a rapid pace. Jax hung back to make sure Alex and I were keeping up. I wondered when that bullet wound was going to catch up to him, and hoped it happened after we reached the promised choppers rather than before.

Alex was gray-faced and stoic as she stalked along next to me, gun held steady in the hand that wasn't a twisted mess of broken bones. I was mildly jealous that she at least had a prisoner's uniform to wear. Breaking out of a Committee torture facility buck-ass naked might make for a good drinking story some-day, but the actual reality kind of sucked. For one thing, it was goddamned cold in here. Or possibly I was going into shock. Hard to tell which.

We met a few guards along the way, alone or in pairs, but there wasn't nearly as much of an organized defense as I might have expected. It made me wonder how many Jax and the others had killed on the way in. I also wondered how long it would take Sloane to call for outside assistance. I didn't know enough about the distribution of Committee assets in this part of the country to even hazard a guess.

After a more intense shootout that winged the hyena guy on the right arm, we broke through and entered what looked like an administrative area. It seemed to be deserted—at least until we came to the open door of a stairwell and saw the bodies piled inside. All but one was wearing the blue uniform of prison staff. The other was dressed in black.

One of the soldiers who hadn't spoken before cursed sharply in a foreign language, and I guessed it was someone he knew.

Above us, the way appeared to be clear. We just had to climb god knew how many flights of stairs to get where we were going. I was already operating in that physically detached sort of way where your muscles did their own thing, despite whatever injuries your brain was ignoring in the heat of the moment.

There were limits, though—and after we'd made it up three flights and part of a fourth, Alex gasped. She was behind me and in front of Jax, who was bringing up the rear. By the time I whirled to see what was happening, Jax had already caught her around the waist and was hauling her right arm across his shoulders to support her.

"Go," he growled, dragging her up the stairs with no regard to the bullet hole in his thigh or the nerve damage that had weakened his left side.

I went, ignoring the gray fog edging into the corners of my vision. The bruises on my face throbbed, and my legs were getting the numb, rubbery feeling that meant they weren't going to keep working forever.

After what felt like an eternity, we burst through a twisted metal security door and into daylight. The sudden brightness brought tears to my one functioning eye. While I tried to blink the blurriness away, a familiar hand clamped around my shoulder and propelled me in the right direction, toward one of the looming dark blurs. The engine noise was deafening, and the rotors had already spun up, generating a powerful downdraft as we crossed the final few yards.

More hands grabbed me and pulled me inside. I twisted to make sure Alex and Jax were aboard as well.

"Where's Beckett?" Jax shouted, pitching his voice to be heard above the racket.

"On one of the other choppers!" someone shouted back.

"These two need stretchers!" Jax said.

After the confirmation that Beckett was safe, I'd already heard everything I needed to hear. With a sense of exhausted relief, I let my knees buckle. My surroundings went black before my body had a chance to hit the metal deck.

TWENTY

Jax

THE PAIN OF the bullet wound in my thigh hit me once Alex and Flynn were safely strapped into their stretchers and having their injuries assessed. Blood was oozing from my wound but not pulsing, despite the strain of half-carrying Alex up the final couple of flights in the stairwell. That alone told me it hadn't hit anything vital.

One of the soldiers cut a slit through the heavy fabric of my trousers to check it, and confirmed it was barely more than a graze. The man slapped a gauze pad over it and gave it a perfunctory bandaging job, after which I put it out of my mind as unimportant.

We'd gotten them out. All three of them. Now that the rush of battle was fading, I had no choice but to start thinking about what came next. What would I be delivering them into?

My headset crackled to life with the tinny sound of the pilot's voice. "We've got enemy choppers incoming. Strap in and get ready for an interesting ride."

Right. Maybe I'd spoken too soon. Apparently, Sloane's cavalry was about to arrive.

The Black Hawk lifted into the air, spraying a final hail of machine gun fire over the section of the compound on our port side. No doubt the other two helicopters were doing the same. Within moments, we were gaining altitude and angling toward the coast, with the Gulf of Mexico beyond.

"Are they armed with missiles?" asked a voice I didn't recognize—probably whoever was in charge in the absence of Irina and Kowalczyk.

"Can't tell," the pilot replied over the comms. "I expect we'll find out soon enough."

This had always been a possibility. To be fair, it could have been worse; if they'd managed to scramble military jets instead of helicopters, we'd be screwed. As it was, it would be a straight-up horse race. If we had more fuel than they did... if they weren't armed with weapons that could be used at long range... if we weren't appreciably slower than they were... if all of those things were true, we might get out unscathed.

"Range is an estimated forty-five nautical miles," said a voice that I tentatively identified as the copilot. "Calculating the pursuing choppers' flight speed now..."

I waited with everyone else, trying not to hold my breath.

"Pursuing aircraft are traveling at one hundred sixty knots," said the copilot.

I wracked my brain for the Black Hawk's specs, but the pilot saved me the trouble.

"Our top sustained cruising speed is one hundred fifty-two knots. I can punch it up to 159 knots if you don't mind guzzling fuel. Orders?"

There was a brief pause, and then the soldier who appeared to be nominally in charge now said, "Punch it. If they get close enough to shoot us down, fuel won't matter."

It was the right call… unless we ended up having to ditch this bird in the ocean after running out of gas. I felt the slight increase in g-force as the chopper sped up.

"Choppers Two and Three are accelerating to match us," the pilot said. "The hostiles can still catch us, but it will take them a while at this speed."

My headset went silent as everyone in the helicopter shut up and strapped in, waiting to see how things would play out. I'd taken a seat near the two stretchers laid out on the deck, and I passed the time watching the slow rise and fall of my packmates' chests.

Slightly less than an hour later, the copilot's voice came over the headsets again. "Enemy choppers are within firing range. Repeat, enemy choppers are within firing range. No missiles detected, but we're taking machine gun fire. Do we engage?"

"Negative," said the de facto commander. "We don't have the fuel for a battle. Attempt evasive maneuvers, but keep heading for the base at top speed."

I wasn't sure what evasive maneuvers he thought the pilot would be able to manage without significantly altering course. Then again, no one had asked me. The helicopter dipped and swerved, my stomach struggling to play catch-up.

"Chopper Three is hit!" the pilot reported. "Smoke from the main rotor assembly! Taking evasive action to give them space to maneuver!"

The pilot banked into a steep turn to the port side, and we all scrambled for purchase.

"It's no good!" he called. "They're in a spin. They're going down!"

Through the windows on the opposite side of the fuselage, I saw the horrible sight of a helicopter spiraling crazily, smoke pouring from the main engine, its trajectory headed for the unforgiving sea below. My heart jumped into my throat.

"God*damn* it!" the commander cursed. "Status of the pursuing choppers?"

There was a painful pause. Then, "Pursuing craft are changing course. They're... they're turning back, sir. Must have hit the edge of their range."

Depending on where they'd started from, they could easily have utilized half of their fuel supply by now if they weren't outfitted for long-range service. They would have to head back or risk the same watery fate that had just befallen Chopper Three. And right now, I didn't give a flying fuck about any of that.

"Which helicopter was Beckett on?" I asked hoarsely, barely recognizing my own voice.

"Chopper Two," the commander replied grimly.

The steel band around my chest snapped, and I sucked in a wheezing breath of air.

Respectful silence reigned for the rest of the trip, broken only by necessary communication between the pilot and copilot. It felt like an age before the sandy browns and vibrant greens of Cuba appeared before us, more welcome than I ever would have guessed they'd be.

Please, just let us get down safe, I thought. *Get us back to Leona and Kam, and let all six of us survive this nightmare for another day. We'll deal with the rest when it comes.*

Numbly, I watched the ground get closer and closer, until the Black Hawk touched down with a dull thump. Through the windows, I saw Chopper Two land safely nearby, and breathed a sigh of relief. Both helicopters' engines powered down with a low whine, leaving us once more inside Kostya Nikolayev's territory.

I tried to take stock. I was still armed, but with Flynn and Alex unconscious, all I'd be able to accomplish with a single handgun was getting myself—and possibly them—killed. We were still trapped. I needed to make sure the others got medical treatment for whatever was wrong with them. I'd seen Alex's left hand before one of the soldiers had bandaged it to immobilize the broken fingers. The memory made me long for a neck to break, the same way Flynn had broken the lab tech's.

Once I was sure the others were being cared for, I needed to find Leona and Kameron, to confirm they were safe and let them know what was happening. My hand shook with adrenaline fatigue as I reached for the clasp of my safety harness and unlatched it. Both side doors on the fuselage slid open, revealing several figures hurrying toward us. Neither Alex nor Flynn stirred in response to the commotion; no more than they'd stirred when we were being shot at earlier. I positioned myself in front of them. Anyone coming for them would have to answer my questions first.

Before long, the soldiers had cleared out and two men wearing the uniforms of Nikolayev's prison guards stepped in. Interestingly, they were unarmed.

"Stop," I said. "These two need urgent medical attention. Are they going to get it?"

The one on the left looked at me like I was an imbecile. "Of course they are," he said in a pronounced German accent. "There are alphomic specialists waiting outside. Now if you would please move so we can get them off the helicopter?" He glanced at my leg. "And have someone direct you to the medical building to get that seen to once you've been debriefed."

I moved aside reluctantly, watching with an eagle eye as the broad-shouldered pair lifted Flynn's stretcher and carried him outside. A second pair came in immediately afterward and did the same with Alex. I followed them out, favoring my left leg heavily and silently cursing the asshole who'd shot me.

Flynn was already being transferred to a gurney, with Alex close behind. We were losing the light. Nearly a whole day had passed since Leo had been taken away after breakfast for her private meeting with Nikolayev, and then come back afterward to talk me into helping with this mission.

Had it been a mistake? I still didn't know the answer, but after seeing what had been done to my packmates in the handful of days since they'd been captured, it was hard to think so.

Medical staff in white coats leaned over Alex and Flynn, pressing stethoscopes to their chests and carefully palpating their ribs. Marginally reassured that they weren't going to immediately be hauled off for more torture, I turned my attention to the second helicopter. Something occurred to me, and I stopped a passing soldier.

"Was Irina on that chopper? Or was she on the one that went down?" I asked.

"She was on that one," the soldier replied. "She's gone to make a report."

"Thanks," I said, not particularly caring if she were dead or alive on my own behalf. Still, I could only imagine that the fallout from Alex learning about all of this would be even worse if I had to tell her that her former mate had miraculously survived execution, only to fall into the ocean in a burning chopper after helping to rescue her. At least I could spare her that much.

The next order of business was Beckett. It seemed to be taking a long time for them to bring him outside, and my worry spiked as I approached the helicopter and heard the sound of animal snarling coming from within.

It was the sound of a cornered omega.

I didn't think—I just charged inside, grabbing at the edge of the doorway for support when my leg threatened to give out.

"Get away from him," I growled at the two betas trying to approach the stretcher. When they didn't respond immediately, I pulled out my gun and pointed it at them. "I said back away *now!*"

They backed away, hands raised. At the same instant, the scent hit me.

Lavender and peppermint. I'd never smelled it before, and yet I felt like I knew it intimately. It was the scent of the carrier-figure I'd never had until I was already a grown man... a scent that said *family*. And it was pungent with heat markers.

"We think he's been drugged with sodium thiopental," said one of the betas, still holding his hands up. "Sloane's been known to use it to loosen prisoners' tongues, but he's reacted badly to it."

Maybe they couldn't smell it yet. *Fuck*—Beckett wasn't anywhere near due for a heat right now. But he also wasn't young anymore. He was approaching estropause, and omegas' systems could get a little crazy as they started to shut down. Could the drug have sent him into an off-cycle heat?

I holstered the gun, since the two men didn't seem like a threat. "Seriously, just back off. I know him; we're like family. I'll try to calm him down and get him outside, but he needs a *specialist*, you hear me? A specialist in omega medicine."

Again, I received that look—like I was a few screws short of a full set.

"Yes, the doctors are waiting outside for him," said the one on the right.

I nodded and gave them a jerk of my chin that clearly said *'please fuck off now.'* They fucked off, somewhat to my surprise. When Beckett and I were alone in the cabin, I scooted carefully down the wall into a sitting position with my injured leg held straight out in front of me, so I wouldn't be looming over him.

"Hey, Boss," I said quietly. "Sorry I was late."

God, he looked horrible—like a man who'd seen into the mouth of hell and barely lived to tell the tale. His heat-scent was sour with stress and fear. It wouldn't have affected me regardless—we might not have been blood-related, but we'd become family long ago. I tried to regulate my emotions into something reassuring, despite the fact that the only thing I could think of worse than placing him in Nikolayev's hands in the first place, was doing so when he was helpless in heat.

Pale, bloodshot eyes the color of a stormy sea met mine, the barest hint of recognition lighting them. Relief eased the tension in my shoulders.

"There you are, Boss. Come on—aren't you just dying to read me the riot act for taking so long to come and get you? Flynn and Alex are here, too... in case no one told you yet. They're getting checked over by the doctors, and you need to do the same."

I thought I could see a flicker of understanding behind that stormy gaze, but then a commotion outside interrupted. Beckett's eyes went wild again, and he jerked violently at the velcro cuffs restraining his wrists to the rails of the stretcher.

"Easy now—" I began, only to be cut off by shouts from outside.

"*Sir! Sir! You mustn't go in there yet... there's an alpha inside—!*"

The clang of rapid footsteps on metal decking echoed through the fuselage. An aura of promised violence reached me the instant before Kostya Nikolayev appeared at the far end of the cabin, his hair disheveled and his lips curled back in a wordless snarl.

Every instinct I possessed had me upright in a heartbeat despite the bullet wound in my leg and the weakness in my muscles. In a flash, I was standing protectively in front of Rhys Beckett, drawn up to my full height... my muscles bulging with threat.

"*Get. Out,*" Nikolayev hissed. His voice didn't even sound human.

"You child-murdering *fucker*," I growled. "Take one more step, and we'll see if I can rip your head clean off your spine before any of your lackeys can put a bullet through my skull."

Gray eyes glowing with rage, Nikolayev stalked forward.

TWENTY-ONE

Leo

I RAN AFTER Irina and Kam, huffing and puffing as I tried not to fall too far behind. Irina had retrieved us from our cell only moments ago. She hadn't told us anything beyond the fact that they had *'successfully retrieved the targets.'*

Two huge black helicopters sat on the pavement that apparently served as the compound's helipad. Dozens of people milled around them. Several were gesturing and shouting in Russian. Confusion and chaos reigned.

Irina collared a man in a white coat who was standing next to an empty gurney. "What's happening?" she demanded.

"He went charging in there after Beckett, but one of the alphas was already inside," the man replied in clipped tones, gesturing toward the nearest helicopter.

"Who went in? Nikolayev?" Irina said in a tone of foreboding, and the man nodded.

"*Fuck!*" she cursed, and charged toward the helicopter.

My stomach dropped. Kam and I exchanged a wide-eyed look and followed her up the metal ramp that had been placed beside the chopper's open side door. Our footsteps clanged loudly.

An idea so improbable that I could scarcely credit it had been percolating through my mind during the course of this endless day of waiting. I hadn't said anything to Kam, since I had no proof—and more than a hint of suspicion that the stress was finally getting to me, making me see patterns that weren't there.

But when we skidded to a stop behind Irina and got a look inside the cabin, I knew with utter certainty that I was right.

"Sir!" Irina said, lunging forward and wrapping her fingers around Kostya Nikolayev's arm. "Sir, please! Just stop for a minute! He's only trying to protect—"

Nikolayev *growled*.

At the far end of the cabin, Jax stood poised in front of a struggling figure on a stretcher. The alpha's fists were clenched, and blatant desire for murder lit his blue eyes. A faint hint of mint and lavender wafted to my nose, the pleasant scent overlaid with the sourness of fear and desperation.

"Oh my god," Kam breathed.

"Jax!" I cried. "Step away from him—you don't understand!"

Screwing up my courage, I held my breath and squeezed past Irina and Nikolayev toward the front of the cabin. I clamped a hand around

Jax's arm the same way Irina had grabbed the Russian's.

Jax bared his teeth and tried to shove me behind him, but I set my feet, refusing to budge.

"I'll kill him before I let him lay one hand on Beckett," he snarled, his eyes never leaving Nikolayev's. "I should fucking kill him anyway."

I grabbed the front of his shirt and pulled on it until he looked down at me. "No! Look at him, Jax! Don't you see? He's Beckett's mate!" I said. "Nikolayev is an alpha—he's the one Beckett's been protecting all this time!"

Jax blinked down at me, a hint of shock breaking through mindless alpha rage.

"Please, Jax," I begged softly. "Get out of his way before he decides to go through both of us."

I could feel the tremor of exhaustion in Jax's muscles, and I hadn't missed the red-stained bandage wrapped around his thigh, either.

"Do as your omega says," Nikolayev ground out, his Russian accent thicker than I'd ever heard it before. "*Now.*"

Kam darted past Irina to join us, taking Jax's other arm. "Let's step into the cockpit for a moment, yes? Unless my nose deceives me, those are heat markers—and while you might be willing to stand between an omega in heat and his mate, I'm *really* not."

Between us, we dragged Jax step by hitching step around the stretcher and into the pilot's area at the front of the aircraft. Kam steadied Jax as he swayed, his left leg threatening to buckle. We pressed him to one side of the small area and caged him in with our bodies. His ragged breathing filled the cockpit as he struggled to take this new twist on board.

Nikolayev yanked his arm out of Irina's grip and was at Beckett's side in three long strides, kneeling next to the stretcher and tearing away the velcro cuffs binding Beckett's wrists to the metal side rails. Beckett let out a tortured noise and dove forward into Nikolayev's arms, burying his face in the Russian's neck and shaking uncontrollably.

Nikolayev held him fiercely and rocked him back and forth, murmuring, "*Solnishko*, my heart—I have you now... it's over. It's over, I promise—your alphas are safe. I have you."

Beckett made another terrible sound and clawed weakly at the back of Nikolayev's suit jacket, grabbing handfuls of the material and holding tight.

My throat closed up, and I had to look away, turning toward Jax's chest. I was peripherally aware of Nikolayev scooping Beckett up as though the smaller man weighed nothing and whisking him away, out of the helicopter.

Jax drew in another shaky breath, his arms coming up to pull Kam and me against him. I hugged back hard.

"He'll be all right now," I said. I *had* to believe that was true. My entire world had just been turned upside down with the confirmation of my crazy theory—but Nikolayev wouldn't allow any harm to come to the man he'd just carried away like he was handling the most expensive and breakable glass.

"When did you realize, *odama*?" Kam asked, pulling back a bit from the three-way embrace.

"I didn't," I said. "I mean, there were some things that weren't adding up, but I wasn't sure until just now." I looked up to meet Jax's dazed expression, hoping desperately that Nikolayev hadn't been lying about the others. "Flynn and Alex—are they okay?"

"No," Jax said hoarsely. "No, they're not. But they're here, and they're alive."

"Then we'll deal with the rest of it as it comes," Kam said. "And speaking of people who obviously aren't okay—you're about to collapse. We saw a man outside who looked like medical personnel. Come on."

By the time we helped Jax hobble outside, there was no sign of the man in the white coat—or of Irina, Nikolayev, or Beckett. We got directions to the medical building from one of the people working on the other helicopter and began the slow trek in that direction.

"So apparently we're not prisoners any-more?" I asked, still trying to rearrange this new revelation into my worldview.

"I think the guy in charge was a bit too distracted to worry about details like that," Kam muttered. As the taller and stronger of the two of us, he was doing the lion's share of the work in keeping Jax upright and moving forward.

"Irina was the one who let us out of the cell," I mused, remembering the way she'd grabbed Nikolayev in the helicopter cabin, holding him back from an alpha killing rage. "She's high up in this secret hierarchy, I'm sure of it."

Jax shot me an alarmed look. "Alex didn't see her when she brought you out to the chop-pers, did she?"

"No," I told him. "We didn't see Alex or Flynn when we came out."

He relaxed. "They must have already been wheeled off to this medical unit. Good."

"So Alex doesn't know about Irina being alive yet?" Kam asked.

Jax shook his head. "Irina was with the team going after Beckett, and she was in the other chopper on the way back. Alex lost con-sciousness before we lifted off, and she hasn't woken up since."

Worry for all three of our alphas pricked at me. I hoped we'd get some answers once we delivered Jax to the doctors.

"That's not going to be a fun conversation for anyone when she wakes up," Kam pointed out.

"No," Jax agreed. "It's not. No more than the *'hey, I've delivered you into Nikolayev's hands, and it turns out he's the one Beckett's been protecting… but I didn't know it at the time'* conversation."

Every few seconds, some new piece of fallout from that particular revelation popped into my head to throw me for a loop again — but right now, Jax, Flynn, and Alex were at the top of my worry list. The rest of it would have to wait, even if waiting felt like standing at the bottom of a snowy pass and expecting an avalanche to fall on my head.

"One thing at a time," I said.

We made it to the squat, unremarkable building beyond the main house that allegedly contained the medical facilities. The armed and uniformed guard stationed in front took one look at Jax and waved us inside.

The interior was basic, but clean and well lit. Darkness had nearly fallen outside, and I blinked a few times to accustom my eyes to the glare of overhead fluorescent lights. Jax waved away the offer of a gurney and instead let the two orderlies take his weight from Kam and me.

"We're staying with him," I said quickly.

"You can come into the ward as long as you keep out of the way," said one of the orderlies.

"That's fine," Kam told him.

We followed them down a hallway that opened into a large area containing perhaps two dozen medical cots, several of which were occupied.

Jax glanced back at us and saw me looking at the carnage. "Sloane's people fought back," he said grimly. "They shot down one of the choppers, too. It was just blind luck that it wasn't one of the ones we were on."

I couldn't afford to think about that too closely—not if I wanted to keep my composure. "You made it, though," I said. "We all made it."

As the orderlies helped Jax to an empty cot, I scanned the room, aware that Jax and Kam were doing the same. My gaze caught on a large, dark-skinned man lying unmoving on a bed in the corner, and my breath hitched.

"It's Flynn," Kam said. "I don't see Alex."

Jax grabbed one of the orderlies by the forearm. "The female alpha with the broken fingers. Where is she?" His tone said they'd better have a goddamned good answer.

"Being prepped for surgery," the man said matter-of-factly. "Her hand is badly injured. It'll need rods and pins."

My gut churned. I tried to tell myself she'd broken it punching some asshole in the jaw... and didn't believe it for a minute.

"Can we see the other alpha who came in?" I pointed at Flynn, who was currently untended.

The orderly's gaze flicked up, following my gesture. "Yeah, go ahead. If he wakes up, call someone over and then try to see how aware he is. There's a possibility of concussion."

"His skull is the hardest part of his body," Jax muttered. "Go on, you two. Go sit with him. I'll be right here for a bit, I'm guessing."

"We'll watch over him," Kam promised.

I wanted to dart forward and kiss Jax first, bless his giant, uncomplicated heart—but I was cognizant of the orderlies' warning not to get in their way while they were working. They were already leaning over him, efficiently removing the makeshift bandage around his leg.

There were no handy chairs nearby, so actually *sitting* with Flynn wasn't really an option. My heart ached as I stood over him, taking in the black and blue of his bruised and swollen face… the small burn marks littering his bare chest. I knelt on the floor and rested an elbow on the edge of the thin mattress, while Kam perched on the edge of the cot on Flynn's other side.

Needing to touch, I reached out and trailed gentle fingers over Flynn's collarbone. "Hey," I whispered.

For a long moment, there was no response… but then Flynn's chest rose and fell on a deep breath.

"Honey and orchard blossoms," he rasped. His right eye blinked open—the left was swollen shut. He gazed blearily between us, and a slow smile tugged at the corners of his split lips. "Now there's a nice way to wake up."

TWENTY-TWO

Leo

"FLYNN," I SAID in relief. My hands hovered, unsure where to land. "I don't know where it's safe to touch you."

He gave a hoarse chuckle and wrapped an arm around my shoulder, tugging me against his chest. I was still worried I'd hurt him if I squeezed back, so I tried to keep my weight as light as possible against him as I soaked up the contact. Spicy musk tickled my nose, soured by stale sweat. I breathed it in deeply anyway.

Kam patted his shoulder, then stood up. "I'll find a doctor."

"Alex and Beckett?" Flynn asked. "They okay?"

"They're here," I hedged, not moving from his embrace. "Alex is in surgery for her hand. Beckett is… a bit more complicated, but I'm pretty sure he'll be okay now. Jax has a hole in his leg, but he seems all right otherwise. He's just across the ward."

Silence fell for a moment, too heavily.

"There's something you're not telling me, sweet thing," Flynn said, proving that his hard skull had apparently done its job of protecting his brain after all. "Is it something I need to know about?"

I pulled back so I could meet his single, bloodshot eye. "It is, but the doctors want to assess you for concussion first. Promise I'll tell you right afterward, okay?"

He gazed up at me with an easy sort of trust that broke my heart. "If you say so, Leona. Just hope they're not planning on asking me any hard questions—I forgot to study for the test."

"If you know what year it is and who the current prime minister is, I think you're probably fine," I told him.

Kam returned with a doctor in tow, and the woman ran through the usual protocol of checking pupillary reaction while asking a few basic questions. When she moved on to ask him if he remembered what had been done to him, my stomach dipped unpleasantly.

"Mostly beatings and electrical torture," he said, as though it wasn't completely horrific. "Got a couple of teeth loose on the right side, and I'm fucking pissed because I'm pretty sure nipple clamps are ruined forever for me now."

"We'll schedule you for dental assessment as soon as you've had a bit more time to rest," the doctor replied, equally matter-of-fact. "And I'm all too familiar with alpha bravado, so I'll see if we can get a trauma specialist in for counseling."

"*Trauma counseling*? Seriously? You've really got all the bells and whistles here, don't you?" Flynn mused. "Does kind of make me wonder where the hell we actually are, though."

The doctor gave a bland smile and left without answering.

"About that," I said, when the three of us were alone again.

"Yeah," he agreed. "About that."

"We found out who Beckett's mate is," Kam said. "And… it's a bit complicated, to put it mildly."

"Also, Irina's alive," I blurted. "Alex doesn't know yet."

Flynn stared at us for a long moment. "Maybe you'd better start from the beginning."

"Right." Kam exchanged a glance with me and cleared his throat. "Shortly after you failed to check in, paramilitary troops stormed the safehouse in the middle of the night and captured us. They flew us to this compound, which is in Cuba, by the way."

We ran through the unlikely sounding story, interrupting each other with various salient points until I finally finished, "And by that point, Beckett was in heat. Nikolayev stormed into the helicopter to get him, which is when we realized that he's the mate Beckett's been protecting all this time."

Flynn continued to stare at us for so long that my eyes watered with the need to blink on his behalf.

"Bullshit," he said eventually.

"Apparently not," Kam told him. "It… mostly adds up, though there are a few questions I'd like the answers to, before we get pulled much deeper into this situation."

There were questions I needed answered, as well. Questions about Nikolayev's dead sister, and the unregistered omegas he'd so famously hunted down for sport on his family's estate in Russia. Questions about how Beckett had ended up mated to the chairman of the Euro-Soviet Committee.

Flynn gave a slow, one-eyed blink. "You said Irina's alive. You absolutely sure about that?"

"Jax is sure," I said. "He knew her before, right?"

"Yeah," Flynn replied after a faint pause. "He did. Shit, that's gonna be Armageddon all on its own, if it's true."

"She's close with Nikolayev, from what we've seen so far," I said. "She also organized the mission to retrieve you."

"Fuck me sideways," Flynn muttered. "Gotta say, this isn't what I expected when I woke up to find you two looking down at me."

"I think I can safely say that none of us expected this," Kam said.

"With the possible exception of Beckett," I couldn't help adding. While I could certainly understand the need for secrecy, Flynn's boss still had some serious explaining to do.

"If Beckett's in an off-cycle heat, it'll be a few days till we get any answers worth a damn," Flynn said. "Can't say I'm real happy about that situation, given that I still don't trust Nikolayev as far as I could throw him. And I don't think I could throw him very far at the moment."

I closed my eyes, remembering the way Beckett had fallen into his mate's embrace in abject relief. "You didn't see them together. Honestly? I think that part of it's just fine."

Flynn let out a wordless grunt, neither agreement nor disagreement.

<hr>

Alex was in surgery for several hours, which was worrying. When she was finally wheeled out, still unconscious, Jax bullied the staff into placing her in a cot next to Flynn's. He also ignored his own medical orders by getting out of bed to sit with her—but at least that inspired the orderlies to locate a few chairs for us.

Kam offered to take hand-holding duty so Jax could rest, but Jax refused.

"Only because I don't want to risk you ending up with a busted hand, too," he said. "Once I'm sure she's not going to try and murder the nearest person when she wakes up, she's all yours."

Flynn was dozing, his body recovering from the abuse it had taken. The doctors had x-rayed his jawbone earlier, and they at least seemed to think he wouldn't lose the teeth. He was slated for a procedure in the morning to stabilize them, so the stretched ligaments anchoring them to his jaw could have a chance to heal.

In addition to her broken left hand, Alex had been flogged. The slow burn of rage that had kindled in my stomach as the doctor described the damage to her back still hadn't subsided. Flynn had apparently sensed my very un-omegalike fury, because he'd said, "For what it's worth, she shot the guy in the head afterward. *Boom*—exploding skull fragments, brain splatter, the whole nine yards."

That did, in fact, make me feel better... which was objectively a bit worrying. I was supposed to be a diplomat, and diplomats weren't supposed to fantasize about people being killed in horrible ways.

We waited, watching over Flynn and Alex as they slept. I had Flynn's large hand clasped in mine, simply because I couldn't bear not to have physical contact with him after the terrible days of uncertainty.

By unspoken mutual agreement, we didn't discuss any of the recent cataclysmic revelations—or the resulting unimaginable consequences for the underground. Silence reigned in the echoing infirmary, broken only by the occasional snore or cough from one of the injured soldiers sharing the space with us. The lights had been lowered to make resting easier, but there was still enough illumination to allow the nurses to see what they were doing when they came through at regular intervals to check on their patients.

The clock on the wall read two forty-five a.m. when Alex gave a low whine of distress, moving restlessly in her sleep. She'd been placed on her right side to keep the pressure off her injured back, with her left hand in its complicated frame of splints and wires strapped to her chest in a tight sling.

Flynn woke instantly, wincing as he rolled into a sitting position on the edge of the cot. We all turned toward her, watching closely.

"*Alef?*" Jax asked quietly. "It's all right. We're all safe. Beckett, too. Can you open your eyes for us?"

It was so typical of this pack. Alex wouldn't care whether or not *she* was safe unless her packmates were as well—and Jax knew that. Her back was to me, but I heard her sharply indrawn breath; saw her shoulders tense as she became more aware of her surroundings. Kam, who'd been seated at the foot of her cot, rose and came to stand behind Jax's shoulder.

"Hello, alpha," he said. "Jax tried to mate me while you and Flynn were gone. Please don't break his fingers, though. There's enough of that going around as it is."

That seemed to do the trick, as far as snapping her out of her instinctual panic. Her head shot up.

"Jax did *what*?" she demanded, her voice a bare rasp.

I gave Flynn's hand a final squeeze and grabbed the cup of water sitting on the tray table between the cots, going to join the others.

Jax shot Kam a confounded look. "Not exactly the most pressing issue, I'd've thought."

"It was a misunderstanding, anyway," Kam said magnanimously. "No harm done." He took the cup from me. "Here. Mind your hand, though. And your back. And anything else that hurts, for that matter."

Alex gave both him and Jax wary looks as she let Kam slip the straw between her lips. She drank a few sips and pulled back, craning down to look at the hardware strapped around her damaged hand.

"How do you feel?" Jax asked.

Alex's green gaze turned inward for a moment. "Like shit," she replied succinctly. "Flynn?"

"Right here," Flynn said. "Nice one earlier, with the 'playing possum' thing. Gonna have to remember that for next time."

Alex craned around, reassuring herself that Flynn really was all right. "Beckett?" she asked.

"He's being looked after," I said.

Her eyes narrowed. "I don't like that phrasing."

"We found out the complicated way who his mate is," Jax said. "It's Kostya fucking Nikolayev, Alex. He's a *goddamned alpha*, hiding right at the top of the Committee."

And…wow. No coddling happening here, was there?

There was a longish pause. "I'm still drugged," Alex said uncertainly.

"Yeah, you are," Jax agreed. "But you heard that right, all the same." He hesitated. "And there's something else."

"Jax, *no*," I burst out. This was *not* the right time, hard on the heels of dropping the Nikolayev bomb on her. She looked awful — gray-faced and dazed.

It had been the wrong thing to say. Her hazy gaze sharpened — a hound hot on the scent trail.

"What is it?" she demanded. "Tell me."

Jax took a slow breath. "It's Irina, Alex. She's here. She's alive."

TWENTY-THREE

Leo

ALEX SHOOK HER head slowly back and forth. "No. No, she's dead. I felt her die." Blank incomprehension morphed into flat denial behind her unfocused green gaze.

"You felt the bond break," Kam said softly. "They took her mating gland, Alex—just like they tried to take mine. That was why the bond snapped."

"I—" She cut herself off. Shook her head again, though there was no conviction behind the gesture this time. "But, we didn't... she wasn't..." Again, she trailed off. A painful silence stretched for the span of several heartbeats, before she asked in a wavering voice, "The pups?"

Jax sighed heavily. "I'm sorry, *alef*. They're gone."

I wanted to cry the tears Alex couldn't, like I'd done for her back in Romania. They burned at the backs of my eyes, but I didn't let them spill. This time, I didn't think they'd help.

"I have to see her," Alex whispered. "If she's here, I need to see for myself."

"She led the retrieval mission to get you, Flynn, and Beckett back," Jax said. "But she's been avoiding you so far. During the mission, it was because that kind of distraction could easily have turned deadly. Now, I'm not sure why she still hasn't come. She could still be in debriefings. It's the middle of the night, though… and none of us know where her quarters are located. Or even if we're still supposed to be prisoners, for that matter."

Alex's breathing had grown uneven as she struggled with whatever emotions she was experiencing in reaction to the blunt revelation.

"Then leave me alone, all of you." The words emerged as an angry snarl, but the unsteadiness behind them was unmistakable.

"We're not leaving you alone, *alef*," Jax said.

A dangerous edge sharpened Alex's glare. Flynn had no way to see it from his position behind her, but he must have sensed it somehow.

"Oh, just fuck off back to your cot, Jax. Not all of us want to dissect every little goddamned thing. Let the woman have some privacy if she wants it."

Jax shot him a frustrated look, but he must have decided it wasn't an argument worth having tonight. We were all exhausted—and if Kam and I were exhausted, I could only imagine how much worse it must be for the alphas.

"Fine," Jax said. "We'll deal with things tomorrow. Like you said, it's not like we're going to get any useful answers for another few days. I'm sorry I pushed, Alex. Try to get some rest."

Alex didn't reply. She looked like a trapped animal, ready to gnaw off an injured limb if it meant she could escape. Part of me wanted to venture outside and search for Irina, just so Alex would stop looking like that—but it was three in the morning, and the compound was teeming with armed guards who might or might not assume I was still supposed to be in a cell.

"I'll ask one of the nurses if there's a way to get a message to Irina," I told her.

Alex gave a single, tight nod, meeting my gaze with something like gratitude for the barest instant before she squeezed her eyes shut and turned her face into the cot's thin pillow.

Jax still looked like he wanted to stay at her side. I nudged his shoulder until he rose with a grumble and hobbled back toward his cot. As promised, I found a nurse and asked for the message to be delivered, requesting Irina's presence in the infirmary at her earliest convenience.

Reluctant as I was to be separated from the alphas by even such a small distance as a different cot, the reality was that the blasted things were *not* built with two people in mind—particularly when one of those people was over six feet tall and built like a tank. Two smallish omegas were a different story, though. When Kam gestured me toward the empty cot he'd claimed next to Jax, I went along willingly. And if I had to climb half on top of him to keep from falling off? Well, neither of us was complaining.

———————◆———————

I woke a few hours later feeling as though I'd been up until three in the morning and then slept double with someone on a narrow shelf—not surprising, under the circumstances. I desperately wanted a shower. Actually, I desperately wanted a shower, an appointment with my hair stylist in Montreal, a new wardrobe, makeup, and a manicure.

Somehow, none of those things seemed terribly likely.

Kam, who was very nearly as high-maintenance as I was, hadn't fared much better. His hair stuck out at ridiculous angles, and he had dark circles under his dark circles. I considered commiserating with him about the lack of amenities, but that thought was completely derailed when a slender figure wearing the uniform of Nikolayev's private guard entered.

Irina's gray eyes swept around the bustle of the medical ward. They caught on Alex's back for a long moment. Alex didn't stir—proof, if any were needed, that their bond was truly destroyed. If it hadn't been, her mate's arrival would have woken her from the soundest sleep.

Eventually, Irina wrenched her gaze free and approached Kam and me.

"Good morning," she said in a cool tone. "I've arranged for more suitable accommodations where you and your alphas can recover, once they've undergone any additional treatment they may need for their injuries."

At the sound of her voice, Alex did wake. She stiffened on her cot, drawing in an audible breath.

"Thank you," I replied uncertainly. "And thank you for coming here. Alex wants to speak with you."

"I'll just bet she does," Irina murmured. Then, more conversationally, "Someone will be along shortly to show you to your suite. Until then, there's a continental breakfast set up in the nurses' staff room, I believe."

With that, she turned with military precision and moved to Alex's cot. Kam and I watched with trepidation. Meanwhile, Jax and Flynn were both still out cold thanks to a combination of physical and mental exhaustion topped with painkillers.

"Is this going to be all right, do you think?" Kam asked.

"I have absolutely no idea," I told him truthfully.

TWENTY-FOUR

Alex

THAT VOICE. I knew that voice. It had been a part of me once—the other half of my whole. And it was here, in this place that should have been a house of horrors, but that we were now supposed to believe was a haven.

Irina Pasternak. The omega I'd mated, pupped, and then lost to the Committee. She was speaking to Leona McCready, mere yards away. Discussing accommodations, her voice as cool and unaffected as though she were nothing more than Nikolayev's pet soldier. As though she hadn't once been... *mine.*

I could hardly breathe for the pain of it.

Leona was thanking her for coming... because I'd demanded to see her. Because I hadn't really believed it was true. I wasn't entirely sure I believed it now. What were the odds I was still in Sloane's interrogation room, unconscious and delirious from my injuries? Perhaps the rest of this had all been a dream?

More low voices, and then footsteps approached. I would have to open my eyes and look soon. Any second. Any second now...

The boots stopped beside my cot. I couldn't scent her. They'd taken everything that had made her an omega. That had made her *my* omega. They'd taken our *pups*. I tensed the muscles in my broken hand, pulling against the pins and stitches holding bones and ligaments together—using the pain in an attempt to ground myself.

"Alex," she said.

I opened my eyes. My former mate stood before me. She looked much as she always had—serious gray eyes too large for her elfin face, honey-blonde hair done up in a regulation twist. But there were new lines around her eyes and at the corners of her lips, just as there were around mine.

"Well, this is awkward," she said.

There was a heavy beat of silence.

"How can you be here?" I asked. "How is any of this real?"

"I imagine it's all a bit of a shock," she agreed. With a quick frown, she glanced over her shoulder. "Let's have this conversation somewhere more private. I assume you can walk?"

My hand itched like termites were crawling beneath the skin. My back was a blank canvas of drugged numbness that whispered *bad*. But my legs seemed fine. I heaved myself into a sitting position on the edge of the cot, finding my balance slightly off thanks to one arm being strapped against my chest.

Irina stepped back, giving me space as I rose on unsteady legs. The room stopped spinning after a few seconds, so I gave her a cautious nod.

"This way," she said, and headed toward a door in the back of the infirmary.

I followed, being careful of my body in a way I'd never needed to before. I'd been injured from time to time, of course—but never like this. I'd never had to be stitched and patched back together with steel pins and thread.

I really wasn't enjoying it so far.

Irina led the way to what seemed to be an examination room. It was unoccupied and had a lock on the door, which she engaged. I sat down in the single chair, mostly because trying to stand held the possibility of a humiliating collapse at some point. Irina leaned hipshot against the functional row of cabinets that held a sink and several drawers.

"You have questions," she said. "I can't answer all of them, but I'll answer what I'm able to."

I couldn't read her face or body language, and that was new. No unregistered omega managed to sneak into the armed services without being an exceptional actor, but she'd never hidden herself from *me*. Fresh disquiet rose in my chest.

Questions. Where to even start?

"How?" I asked, the single word encompassing most of what I was so desperate—and terrified—to hear.

Her chest rose and fell on a deep breath. "How did I survive?"

I nodded.

"Nikolayev was not yet the Chairman when I was arrested, but he was an up-and-comer with a reputation for viciousness," she said. "I assume the others have already told you that he's a plant. The underground's most valuable mole, hiding in plain sight."

"He's a monster," I said, because I hadn't even *begun* to process the idea of Nikolayev being Beckett's mate yet.

"He has spent a lifetime cultivating the persona of a monster," she replied carefully. "There's much more you still don't know, but everything he's done has been in service of the cause of alphomic resistance."

"At what cost, though?" I muttered, thinking of all the dead alphas and omegas.

"Less than you think, and more than many would be willing to pay," she shot back. "Anyway, my family and I were immigrants. You already know this."

I nodded. They'd come from the Ukraine when Irina was nine. She'd lost much of her accent, but not all of it. Now, it was more pronounced than I remembered.

"What you don't know is that my mother was friendly with Sofia Nikolayev, Kostya's sister, when they were at university together."

"Nikolayev's sister... the one he killed when she presented as an omega in adolescence?" I asked skeptically. "That doesn't add up."

"Yes." Irina let out a little huff of dark amusement. "Such a shocking act of violence, wasn't it? They say the body was *practically unrecognizable* when he was finished with her."

The words clicked into place, and I blinked. "You're telling me he faked a murder? Of his own *sister*?"

"The family did, yes. Sofia Nikolayev is now Sofia Shevchenko, married to a beta soviet chancellor in the Ukraine. Together, they are the nominal leadership of the underground in that area—and congratulations, because you now possess information that could bring down a sizable chunk of the resistance. Not to mention a sizable part of the Ukranian government."

I shook my head, trying to settle everything into place through the haze of pain, exhaustion, and drugs. "But your arrest. That doesn't explain—"

"I told you my mother had a connection to the Nikolayev family," Irina said. "When I disappeared, she used it. The Committee's extradition laws are draconian. The fact that I was born in the Ukraine was grounds for the Euro-Soviet Committee to have me hauled back there. I was a special case, you see. I'd infiltrated the beta military. Such an egregious offense brought me to Kostya's personal attention, and we all know what he does to omegas on his family's private estate." Her voice dripped with irony.

"Your trial and execution records were sealed," I said hoarsely.

She shrugged. "Of course they were. Stories of hunting down prisoners in the forest like animals play well with the zealots, but it makes for messy paperwork. Especially when those prisoners are actually disappearing rather than dying."

"But our pups." My throat felt tight around the words. "He *mutilated* you! Our bond..."

Real anger flared in her eyes. "He did no such thing!" she snapped. "He was just... a bit too slow."

She looked away, her hand lifting to brush fingertips over her lower abdomen. It was the first unintentional body language I'd seen from her. "I've no doubt the bastards who violated me assumed I'd die of shock and blood loss on the flight across the Atlantic. That's probably why they didn't fight the extradition harder."

My good hand clenched into a fist against my thigh as I pictured it—my nails digging crescents into the flesh.

"Kostya hid me away on his estate," Irina continued in a detached tone. "He got me medical care, and when I'd recovered to the extent it was possible to do, he asked me if I wanted to fight for him from inside the very organization that is trying to destroy us. I said yes."

"You let me think you were dead," I whispered.

She looked suddenly very tired. "Of course I let you think I was dead. What did you expect me to do? Mail you a letter explaining that a high-ranking member of the Committee is also a high-ranking member of the underground, and that he'd saved me so I could work for him? That was never going to happen."

My head was spinning with more than the painkillers now. "But Beckett—"

"Is Nikolayev's mate," she said sharply. "And you were not in his confidence when it came to that fact."

That was a knife straight to the gut—a brutal reminder that Beckett hadn't trusted us enough to tell us more than the bare minimum we needed for any given mission.

Irina must have seen something of this in my expression, because she continued in a gentler tone. "He did it to protect you."

A rusty sound emerged from my throat—the opposite of a laugh. "Yes. And look how well that's worked out for everyone involved."

Irina's expression closed off again. "You're all here. You're alive. There are worse outcomes."

"So what does this mean for us?" I demanded, needing to know what she expected of me now that this years-long charade was finally ending.

Her faunlike brows drew together. "It means nothing for us, Alex. I'm sorry—but we were adolescents and we didn't have the faintest idea what we were doing. I was in heat and I begged you to bite me, and in the heat of the moment, you did. You didn't want a mate-bond any more than I did, once the hormones wore off."

I stared at her, stunned.

She stared back, unblinking. "Look me in the eye and tell me you wanted me to get pregnant any more than I wanted to *be* pregnant. For god's sake, Alex, that's why we used contraceptives in the first place."

"I would have protected those pups with my life!" I told her, appalled at her implication.

"That's not the question I asked," she replied evenly.

My mouth worked for a few seconds before words formed.

"I still don't know what you expect to happen now," I said, trying to drag the conversation onto some sort of footing I could control. If she would only tell me what I was supposed to do with this mate-bond that wasn't... I could do it. I could take *action*, instead of this terrible uncertainty and guilt.

The look she gave me was very nearly pitying. "Alex, I don't expect anything to happen now, except that you'll be grieving for someone who's alive rather than someone who's dead."

"Irina. I don't understand what you're saying." Even I could hear the hint of desperation creeping into my voice.

"I'm with someone," she said. "I'm in a relationship that makes me happy. He doesn't make me feel as though my lack of a mating gland or a womb makes me somehow incomplete as a person. And..." She paused and glanced away, unable to meet my eyes. "... he isn't a constant reminder of a past I would rather forget."

I blinked at her, trying to force the sense of the words through a blank wall of incomprehension.

She wasn't finished, though. "Don't live in the past, Alex. You have a future waiting, too. You just have to reach out and take it."

I tried to say something. *Anything*. I couldn't. There was a great upswell of something ugly and putrid growing inside me, and I knew I couldn't be in this room when it burst free. I rose from the chair without a word, unlocked the door, and left—ignoring the call of "*Alex, wait—!*" from behind me.

TWENTY-FIVE

Leo

WHEN IRINA HAD said '*more suitable accom-modations*,' I'd mostly been hoping for something that didn't involve heavy locks and security doors. I hadn't expected the entire ground floor of the east wing in the spectacular main house.

We were shown to the rooms by someone I could only describe as a butler—a tall, stooped older man missing one arm and an eye. He gave us the guided tour, announcing the purpose of each room in a precise German accent. When we'd completed the trek through bedrooms, bathrooms, fully stocked kitchen, dining room, living room, and yes, a nest, he turned to face us, his tone and expression grave.

"I must ask you not to venture into the west wing. Chairman Nikolayev is currently sequestered there with his mate, and he does not wish to be disturbed."

"We understand," I said, equally gravely. "We have no wish to interrupt our host and his mate during this private time."

I wasn't entirely sure the two alphas behind me agreed with the sentiment, but they'd be bothering Beckett during his heat over my dead body. We might not have all the answers we wanted, but if there was one thing I had faith in right now, it was the devotion I'd seen between Beckett and his unlikely, impossible mate.

"Then I will leave you to rest," said the probably-a-butler. "If you need assistance with anything, the bell pulls in the rooms are all functional. Use them and someone will come immediately."

"Thank you," I told him. "You've been a great help."

The man bowed formally and departed, leaving us in the lavishly appointed wing of a fully staffed colonial-era mansion in the middle of the Cuban rainforest.

"This is nuts," Flynn said. The words were a bit slurred after the dental surgery he'd just undergone to stabilize his loose teeth, but the meaning was clear enough.

On the one hand, I sympathized with the sentiment. But on the other hand, it made sense, given what we now knew. "Beckett is Nikolayev's mate, and you're practically Beckett's pups," I said. "It's not really that surprising that he'd roll out the red carpet."

"Didn't stop him from tossing us in a cell when we first got here," Jax muttered. He lowered himself onto the sofa of the living room where we'd fetched up at the end of the tour, leaning the cane he was grudgingly using against the armrest.

Kam sat on the other end, his head falling to rest against the back of the couch. "I get the impression that if Beckett hadn't been in heat, Nikolayev wouldn't have let their status as mates slip like he did." He stared up at the pristine white plaster of the ceiling and the intricate gold-painted cornices for a long moment before adding, "And to be fair, it was a very pleasant cell, as cells go."

"I'm amazed he was able to maintain the facade as long as he did," I said. "He must have felt every moment of Beckett's interrogation and torture through the bond." To be able to pretend disinterest while experiencing the pain of the one closest to you in all the world…

I shivered.

Flynn flopped down in an armchair, wincing a bit. Thanks to alpha healing, the swelling on his face was already starting to go down, but he'd still been through the wringer.

Speaking of which—

"I don't like the fact that Alex insisted on separate accommodations," I said.

"No," Kam agreed darkly. "The two of you don't find that worrying at all?"

"Figured she was probably getting reacquainted with Irina," Flynn said.

"Seems likely," Jax agreed.

I turned to him. "I still can't believe you dumped all of that on her with no warning." There was censure in my tone, and I couldn't help it. This had been eating at me ever since Alex woke up.

Jax met my eyes and held them. "Leo, the thing you don't understand about Alex is that she won't accept coddling, and she hates prevarication. Period. If she wanted to be here with the rest of the pack, she'd be here. She was pretty damned clear that she wanted space from us."

"What we want and what we need are often two very different things," Kam said philosophically. He rolled his head up from his perusal of the ceiling. "You could have at least tried to talk to her afterward."

Flynn scoffed.

"Sure," Jax said. "And I could have gotten my ass verbally reamed if she was in a good mood, or punched in the face if she was in a bad mood. She's still got one good hand, you know."

He must have noticed my answering scowl, because he softened a bit. "Alex doesn't do feelings, Leo. Trying to *make* her do them doesn't end well for anyone involved. That's just the way she is. It's not our place to try and change her—not that we'd want to in the first place. She's Alex. She's our *alef*, and she's also an emotionally constipated hardass. A fact that's saved our lives on more than a few occasions."

"I'm gonna tell her you said that," Flynn said, sounding half asleep. His eyes were sliding closed, exhaustion catching up to him again.

"Which part?" Jax asked, frowning with what appeared to be genuine alarm. The only answer he got was a snore.

"You should both get some more rest," I said, resigned to losing the argument for now. If she didn't resurface tomorrow, I'd go track Alex down myself. Maybe I was in the wrong here, and she was shacked up in Irina's quarters making up for lost time like the others assumed. I hoped that was the case, even if the idea brought an odd little pang of loss with it.

Perhaps the feeling was on Kam's behalf. That was probably it.

"I want a shower," the omega in question declared. "In fact, I want *all* the showers. God, I feel grungy."

"Ditto," I agreed, not wanting to be alone with my dark thoughts. "Share with me?"

"Always," Kam agreed. "Jax? Why don't you see if you can get Flynn to the nest? He's going to need spinal readjustment if he sleeps for too long in that chair."

Jax grunted acknowledgement and levered himself to his feet. I got up as well and crossed to kiss him. His lips were soft against mine, and he wrapped an arm around me, pressing my body to his.

"How big is this shower anyway?" he asked, after I broke the kiss.

I raised an eyebrow at him. "Not *that* big. Also, you're not supposed to get the bandages wet."

"Sponge bath later?" he asked.

Kam snorted, and I couldn't help the huff of laughter that escaped.

"Deal," I promised him.

I stepped out of his embrace and went to press a kiss to the less-bruised side of Flynn's face. He hummed and nuzzled sleepily into the contact.

"Go sleep in the nest," I told him. "We'll be along soon."

"'Kay," he mumbled, not truly awake.

Kam and I headed for the hallway with the row of bedrooms. Among other shocks of the day had been the discovery that Nikolayev's soldiers had rescued our packed bags from the safehouse in New York and brought them along when they captured us. Kam's remaining cash after the purchase of the old car was untouched, and the Kali mask I'd bought him shortly after we first met was undamaged.

More importantly, it meant we had clean clothes. When a rummage around the master bathroom unearthed a decent selection of soap, body wash, shampoo, conditioner, and moisturizer, Kam let out an almost orgasmic groan of pleasure and fell forward onto the treasure trove, gathering the bottles to his chest in the parody of an embrace.

"Oh, thank god," he said.

We stripped and squeezed into the shower stall—which would not, in fact, have accommodated an alpha along with us—and washed each other with the sort of relief that only grimy, high-maintenance omegas could appreciate. When I reached the half-healed bite mark at the base of Kam's neck, I paused.

"How are you doing, really?" I asked, brushing soapy fingertips lightly across the raised flesh. "Are you okay with this?"

He slumped forward into my arms, and I leaned into his embrace in turn.

"Yeah," he said. "I am. Really, it's fine. I… kind of like having it there, if I'm honest."

I pressed my lips to his mating gland as I'd done so many times before. It tasted slightly different than I was accustomed to, and the texture of Jax's tooth marks was unfamiliar beneath my tongue. Kam's shudder of pleasure was the same as it always had been, though.

He pressed his face to the base of my neck and breathed in. Even in the shower, I knew he was scenting me.

"I love that you're off the suppressors," he said against my skin. "Please don't go back on them unless there's a good reason."

It was odd, walking around in the sweet haze of my own perfume—but also freeing, somehow. "Okay," I said, and felt his lips curve into a smile where they pressed against me.

We finished washing each other and rinsed off, stepping out of the now steamy shower stall to dry off with thick towels and rub lotion over everyplace that needed it.

"Are you coming to sleep?" I asked, even though it was only mid-afternoon.

Kam took a deep breath and let it out, considering. "I think I need to burn off some nervous energy first. Since we seem to be guests instead of prisoners now, I might go make use of that gym we saw in the rehab wing of the medical building."

I smiled at him, hopelessly fond. "You've turned into one of those people who's addicted to working out and misses it when they can't, haven't you?" I teased.

"Apparently," he said, with a short laugh. "Admit it, though—you love reaping the benefits."

He flexed his left and right pectorals alternately, showing off the sleek dancer's build I love so much in the most ridiculous way possible. I dissolved into undignified snort-laughter and leaned over to kiss his shoulder.

"Busted," I admitted. "And here I thought I was being so discreet about ogling you."

He kissed my neck. "I'm onto you. I've got a sixth sense like that. Go keep our alphas warm. I'll be back after I've worn myself out and had another shower."

"Have fun," I told him. "Try not to intimidate any of the soldiers with your awesome gym bod."

I threw on an oversized T-shirt that I'd shamelessly stolen from Jax's bag of belongings and went to rejoin the others. They were in the nest as promised, already asleep again — but they'd left a me-shaped gap between them in the massive pile of pillows and blankets on the floor.

I dragged a beanbag over and wriggled into that space, reclining with their heads resting on either side of my thighs. That made it convenient to run the fingers of my right hand through Jax's short blond hair, massaging his scalp. Meanwhile, the fingers of my left hand stroked lightly over Flynn's temple, avoiding the worst of the bruising.

Flynn mumbled something unintelligible and threw a possessive arm over my legs. Jax shifted position until his head rested on my thigh rather than next to it. With that, I settled back and closed my eyes, relieved to let the cares of the day fall away.

TWENTY-SIX

Kameron

MY BODY WAS only partly my own, most of the time—but Leo had been right that when I was exercising it, I found a sort of freedom that was hard to come by in other circumstances. It was not the body I'd been born with, but in the gym, it did my bidding and I settled into my skin in a way that was often difficult to achieve otherwise.

I thought maybe sex would eventually become another such conduit to self-acceptance—at least, the kind of sex I'd had during those intense days of Leo's last heat. I prodded at the idea of Alex, who'd understood so much about me without being told, reuniting with the mate she'd thought lost for so long.

I was happy for her, truly. And also honest enough to grieve a bit on my own behalf, in case this meant she wouldn't want anyone else besides Irina. We wouldn't know that until we all had a chance to talk—and unfortunately, talking didn't seem to be Alex's forte. I hoped Irina balanced her in that regard, but the omega woman's cool demeanor when she'd come to us in the infirmary didn't bode well. Honestly, I was worried for Alex… though I doubted she'd appreciate the sentiment.

For now, though, I intended to put everything out of my mind for a bit in favor of exhausting myself.

The gym in the medical building was geared toward patient rehabilitation, but it would work just fine for my purposes with its weights, treadmills, and elliptical machines. The guard at the door waved me in, and one of the nurses I recognized from the overnight vigil with our alphas gave me a pleasant nod of greeting.

No one questioned my presence as I headed deeper into the building. The gym was exactly as I remembered it from our brief visit, when one of the doctors showed it to us and suggested Jax make use of the facility once his wound was a bit more stable.

I entered with my towel thrown over one shoulder and let my eyes wander over the handful of other people present, all of whom seemed to be looking in one direction rather than using the exercise machines. Following their gazes, I froze in place at the sight of a tall, sleek-muscled figure pummeling the ever loving shit out of a punching bag—*one-handed*.

"Oh, no," I whispered, my heart sinking.

Alex's shoulders were hunched, her weight balanced lightly on the balls of her feet. Her hair was loose, hanging in lank, sweaty strands. Blood streaked the back of the simple hospital clothing she wore as the unhealed whip marks on her back bled through the bandages—the wounds no doubt reopened thanks to the violent punches she was throwing right-handed. Her left arm still appeared to be in its sling, thank god, but there was no way the doctors had cleared her for this kind of activity. The sound of the heavy, thumping blows echoed through the gymnasium.

"Alex," I said, appalled. And then, louder. *"Alex!"*

She didn't hear me, or she was ignoring me. With a feral cry of frustration, she redoubled her efforts to reduce the punching bag to a torn mass of leather and stuffing. *Christ*—her knuckles weren't even wrapped. I dragged my eyes away long enough to look at the others in the gym. They seemed at as much of a loss as I was.

"You know her, right? Should we try to stop her?" asked a beta man with a bandaged shoulder.

A sudden, crushing sense of my inability to deal with this situation on my own assaulted me. But I could only imagine what would happen to any beta stranger who dared to get between Alex's fist and that punching bag.

"No," I said. "Just, uh... give her some space and keep an eye on things, please? I'll be back as fast as I can with help."

The guy shot me an *'are you kidding'* look as I turned to leave. I couldn't really blame him, but I was already jogging rapidly through the medical building, toward the front entrance. Maybe I should have flagged down some doctors, but the vision of half a dozen orderlies tackling Alex to the ground and holding her down while someone injected her with a sedative made me want to vomit.

I ignored the startled questions directed at me by the staff as I charged outside and hared back to the main house. I was breathless when I barged into the nest and skidded to a halt just inside the door. Leo jerked awake from a light doze, her gaze turning frightened when she saw the state I was in. Jax and Flynn, fast asleep on either side of her, didn't stir.

I thanked the universe for heavy-duty painkillers, because my instincts said the alphas' presence would only escalate things further. They seemed to have a very rigid idea about who Alex was and what she needed—one that I suspected was no longer accurate.

I lifted a finger to my lips, urging quiet. "I need you at the gym, *odama*. It's Alex—she's there alone, melting down."

Leo's expression immediately morphed from startled fear to empathy and terrible sadness. "Let me find some pants," she whispered. "Write the others a note, will you? I don't want them to wake up and find both of us gone with no explanation."

I nodded, hurrying to the kitchen for paper, a pen, and a bit of scotch tape as she carefully extricated herself from the nest.

Alex alone and having a meltdown at the gym, I scribbled. *Leo and I have gone to calm her down. Will bring her back here afterward. Please don't follow — leave it to us. Kam.*

I took the note back to the nest and taped it to the beanbag positioned between the two men, so it would be right in front of their faces if they woke up. Leo was waiting for me in the hallway, wearing leggings and sneakers beneath an oversized shirt. Her hair was pulled back in a messy ponytail.

We jogged toward the medical building, and that alone told me how worried Leo was, since she *despised* running for any reason. The guard lifted a hand to stop us this time, staring at us with a frown.

"Problem?" he asked.

"I hope not," I said. "We've got a friend inside who just received some bad news. She's upset."

He gave us a skeptical look up and down, but let us in. We hurried through the building to the gym, where the situation hadn't improved in the interim. Blood smeared the leather of the punching bag now, proof of the damage to Alex's unwrapped knuckles.

"Oh, Alex," Leo murmured, pushing past me to move farther inside. She looked around at the uncomfortable expressions on the other people's faces, and let out a sigh. "I'm so sorry," she said. "But could you all give us some privacy for a bit?"

"Not so sure you two should be in here alone with her, ma'am," said the bandaged beta. "She could be dangerous."

"Not to us," Leo replied, with the same air of utter certainty that had turned contentious diplomatic negotiations in her favor and convinced world leaders to change longstanding views to suit her.

The others exchanged uncertain glances, but then the bandaged man shrugged his good shoulder. "If you say so. Yell if you need help."

"Thank you," Leo told him.

I stood out of the way as the others trooped out of the room, leaving us alone with the sound of rapid, heavy blows and ragged breathing. We flanked Alex's sweat-soaked form, giving her a wide berth as we entered her field of vision.

"Go away," she grated past a clenched jaw. Blood spattered in fine droplets from her split knuckles with every devastating impact.

"No," Leo said softly.

Her teeth bared in an audible growl. "Fuck off with your tears and your diplomacy and your goddamned feelings bleeding all over the place. *Leave me alone!*" The last three words were punctuated with three rapid-fire blows. A small split opened in the leather, white wool stuffing peeking through it.

"Shan't," I said, my heart breaking for her. I met Leo's eyes, silently telegraphing the foolhardy thing I was about to do. She nodded agreement.

As one, we stepped forward. I grabbed Alex's bleeding fist in mid-blow, grunting under the impact against my palm and thanking my lucky stars she was already exhausted. At the same moment, Leo slipped between the alpha and the abused punching bag. Alex jerked her hand free with a gasp and stumbled backward, landing flat on her ass. We knelt in front of her, forming three corners of a sweaty and breathless triangle.

She looked terrible. Her face was bloodless and gray, dripping with clammy sweat. Her hair was matted and tangled, hanging loose since she couldn't do anything practical with it one-handed. Her left hand lay against her chest, fingers curled like the legs of a dead spider, caged inside the frame of wires and pins. The smell of night jasmine and sandalwood languished beneath the stench of sweat and festering grief.

"What did Irina do to you?" Leo asked, her voice hard with anger.

Alex stared at her like she was some sort of exotic alien life form. "Nothing," she snarled. "She did *nothing*."

"The hell she didn't," Leo shot back.

"Something obviously happened," I said in a softer tone. "Please tell us."

Flat green eyes speared me. "She did nothing. She… *wants*… nothing." Her voice cracked on the last word.

"Oh," Leo breathed. "You wanted her back, and she… what? Rejected you?"

Alex made an angry, dismissive gesture with her free hand—her fingers bruised and tinged ruby with blood. "Why would she not? It's been years. The bond is broken. She's found another person and no longer wants me."

"I'm so sorry, Alex," Leo said. "I can't imagine how that must—"

"That's not why I'm angry," Alex said, cutting her off with a sharp jerk of the head. "It's as she told me. We were barely more than pups when I mated her. We were a pair of *idiots*."

"Then, what?" I asked carefully.

"You don't understand!" she flared. "You can't understand—no one can!"

"Explain it to us," Leo insisted, in a tone that brooked no argument. "*Tell us*, Alex."

"She was alive!" Alex cried. "My mate was alive, and I didn't come for her!"

"You couldn't have known," I said, taken aback by the pain in that simple declaration.

"But you still blame yourself," Leo said slowly. "If she was dead, then you'd already failed. There was nothing more to be done. But instead…" She trailed off.

"They killed our pups and ripped her body to pieces," Alex said jaggedly. "She was broken and frightened and alone, and I didn't lift a *fucking finger* to find her and save her."

"Does she blame you for that?" I demanded, ready to go give a certain omega a piece of my mind if she'd said any such thing.

"Of course she fucking doesn't," Alex snapped. "She's moved on. She doesn't love me. She never—" The words choked into silence.

Do you love her? I wanted to ask—but Leona was giving me a warning look.

"I would have loved those pups with my last breath," Alex whispered, and perhaps that was an answer, of sorts. "*God.* We were almost—"

A family, my mind supplied, into the blank space. And oh, how intimately I knew that pain. Pups that might have been. A family that might have been.

I lifted a hand toward her, inching forward on my knees, clearly communicating my intention. When my arm came around her shoulders, high enough to avoid the fresh blood seeping through the bandages, she stiffened.

"Don't touch me," she said hoarsely.

I stilled. "Tell me that again like you mean it, and I promise I'll let go," I said, hoping it wasn't a terrible mistake.

Silence fell, broken only by the awful, labored sound of breathing that wanted to be sobs. One heartbeat, two, three—and Alex slumped against me, shuddering. Leo scooted up on her other side and wrapped her between us, being as careful of her broken hand as a mother bird with a newly hatched chick.

"You have a family," Leo said. "You have a *pack*, Alex. Please, let us take you back to them. They need to know that you're hurting."

Alex let out a low moan of pain and leaned into us, trusting us with her weight. We stayed like that for several long moments, just supporting her between us.

"Do you need to see one of the doctors first?" I asked—worried about the damage she might have done to herself.

Alex uncurled enough to glance down at her bruised right hand as though it belonged to someone else, before shaking her head slowly. "It's fine," she rasped.

She let us heft her to her feet on rubbery legs. After a moment, she nodded, and the three of us began the awkward shuffle toward the front door and the huge house across the compound.

It was more or less the mirror image of when we'd dragged Jax to the infirmary, though Alex gained steadiness as we walked, rather than growing weaker. It felt like the short journey took forever, but eventually we entered the east wing to find Flynn pacing restlessly in the foyer while Jax leaned against the wall, looking pale and haggard.

"Shoulda woke us up," Flynn growled. His eyes were for Alex, though. He looked like someone had taken his compass away and handed it back with the needle pointing south instead of north.

"What happened?" Jax asked quietly.

"Rough day all around," Leo said shortly.

"Is it Irina?" Flynn asked.

"Not here," Leo shot back. "Let's go to the nest."

"Bathroom first," I said. "I want to clean up those split knuckles, if nothing else."

"I'm not an invalid," Alex snapped.

"Take a look in the bathroom mirror and tell me that," I retorted.

Jax and Flynn looked like they thought they should be doing something, or saying something, but they had no idea what it was. I hadn't been wrong about them having an unshakable idea of Alex that didn't really match up with the current reality. Leo and I swept Alex toward the bathroom, where we cleaned her up as best we could over her half-hearted protestations.

I still wasn't happy about the fresh bleeding on her back, but removing and rewrapping the bandages would probably make things worse by pulling open the places where the gauze had scabbed to the skin with dried blood. I resolved to drag her back to a doctor in the morning, or perhaps see if one of them would come here for a house call.

We led Alex to the nest when we were finished, where Jax and Flynn were waiting awkwardly. They'd cleaned up as well at some point, their hair damp and most of the day's grime wiped away.

"Will you tell us what happened?" Jax asked again.

Alex shook her head, but Leo plowed right over her. "Irina's moved on. She's with someone else. Alex blames herself for not having known she was still alive and going after her. And she's grieving her pups."

"Oh," Jax said blankly.

"*Fuck*, Alex," Flynn said, running a hand over his close-shorn black hair. "That's some rough shit. You should've said."

"We're sleeping pack-style tonight," I decided. "Alex, lie down."

"I'm not tired," she muttered.

"You're exhausted," I said, kicking off my shoes and leading by example. "Now lie *down*."

I didn't really expect her to give in without a fight. But she slumped to the cushion-strewn floor, as though hearing me say how tired she was made it real for her.

"Get the lights," Leo said, as she lay down on Alex's other side, mindful of her sling.

After the tiniest of hesitations, Flynn crossed to the door and flicked off the lights. A couple of small nightlights came on, casting a soft reddish glow over the room. Flynn came and lay down behind Leo, slinging an arm across her. Meanwhile, Jax lowered himself carefully to the floor on his bad leg, settling in behind me.

Silence settled over the room, broken only by the sound of our breathing—but it wasn't an easy quiet. Eventually, Jax broke it.

"You had no way of knowing she was alive, *alef*," he said, echoing what I'd told Alex in the gym.

I felt Alex swallow. "We're supposed to come after the ones who are lost," she said, barely more than a whisper. "We're always supposed to come for them. *Always*."

I thought of Beckett, Flynn, and Alex coming after us in the terrorist cave in Romania… of all four of them coming to save us when Leo was arrested. Of Jax rescuing Flynn and Alex from Sloane's torture cell.

"Doesn't sound like Irina was lost, though," Flynn said. "Someone *did* come for her. It just wasn't you."

Unexpectedly, a choked sob emerged from next to me. I put my hand on Alex's shoulder. It was shaking.

"It's all right to grieve," Jax said, sounding a bit choked up himself. "I'm sorry we didn't know you were hurting. I wish you'd told us, *alef*."

"There's been no time to grieve," Alex said in a strangled tone.

"There's time now," I said, squeezing gently.

"They killed my pups," she said around tears. "They killed my *pups*."

And then she was crying in earnest, wracked with ugly sobs as she turned blindly toward me. There was nothing to do except hold her—this hard-as-nails alpha who'd carried all her pain inside for years… for a lifetim*e*. Leo curled around her and stroked her hair, murmuring soothing nonsense as Jax and Flynn reached across us to rest their hands on their *alef*'s shoulder and hip.

"This is pack pain," I said, remembering the way my family would gather to mourn a loss when I was small, in the time *before*. "In a pack, you never have to bear such grief alone."

"Never," Jax agreed.

"Never," Flynn echoed.

"Never," Leo whispered.

Alex only sobbed harder, her tears soaking into my shoulder.

TWENTY-SEVEN

Leo

WE SPENT THE next four days with the world locked outside the doors and did nothing but rest, eat, and connect. Alpha healing meant that Flynn's bruising subsided to slowly fading greens and yellows, and the ugly furrow left in Jax's thigh by the passage of a bullet scabbed over.

The doctors tutted over Alex's back and hand when Kam put his foot down and insisted she let them look at her. He'd barely left her side, and I was pretty sure Jax and Flynn's newly solicitous behavior toward their pack leader was slowly driving her insane. I liked to think the pendulum would swing back to more of a happy medium that everyone could live with, given enough time.

I didn't think I'd ever been so lazy in my life. I slept nearly as much as the people who'd been injured — sometimes in the nest, sometimes in the bedroom I'd claimed as mine. I wasn't willing to flaunt it in front of Alex while she was grieving her own loss so sharply — but privately, the sponge baths I'd promised Jax and Flynn had turned into slow, gentle sex on three occasions, twice separately, and once to-gether.

It was a different experience, having the alphas sleepy and passive beneath me as I took my time, caressing skin with slow strokes and taking them inside me with tender care, riding them until they groaned and spilled, knots locking me in place—exactly where I wanted to be.

It was too late to protest that I couldn't mate them, and we all knew it. There was still one thing holding me back, though.

"I'm asking again," Flynn said at one point, when I was draped boneless across his torso. "I warned you I would."

His knot sent shivers of pleasure up and down my spine with each slow breath I took. I pushed up on my elbows so I could look at him, being careful to avoid the raw electrical burns still littering his chest.

"That's playing dirty," I told him, as liquid pleasure shifted and sparkled inside me.

A half-smile tugged at one corner of his lips. "Only way I know how to play, sweet thing."

I sighed, swallowing a moan as the small movement shifted him inside of me. "You al-ready know I'm going to say yes eventually."

The smile widened. "I knew that a long time ago, Leo."

"But I won't break up your pack by only mating you and Jax, leaving Alex out in the cold," I went on, before he could get too smug about it. "For one thing, I'm pretty sure Kam's in love with her, even if he hasn't quite realized it yet. And I... care for her a great deal," I finished, thinking of the noble alpha who blamed herself for not somehow knowing the unknowable and doing the impossible.

Flynn pulled me down and ravished my mouth with a kiss so deep and thorough it left me dizzy. "And that's one of the reasons I love you. Okay, so it's all or nothing. That's also one of my favorite ways to play."

I nodded. "But Alex isn't remotely ready to talk about the subject, much less act on it. Plus, she may have no interest whatsoever in me—though I think she does in Kam."

Flynn looked like he might argue, so I put a fingertip over his full lips, silencing him.

"If she doesn't want me, we can revisit the subject and figure out what that means for all of us," I said firmly. "But she needs to be part of that conversation, and right now she's not in a position for that. You say *all or nothing,* but that's not it, exactly. I'm not a diva. I don't need all of this to be about me. Maybe Kam bridges the gap between Alex and the rest of us. Maybe we have a strategic mating for pack cohesion, even if it's not a love match. Or maybe she never wants to hear the word *'mate'* again. But she needs to have all those choices open."

Flynn gave an easy shrug beneath me. "Course she does. I hear you, Leo. You know me—I'm patient. Just hearing you say yes instead of finding a million words that don't include no makes me happy."

I gave a rueful snort. "Yeah, you were always going to wear me down eventually, weren't you?"

"Yup," he said, taking my waist in his big hands and shifting his hips, drawing a sharp gasp of ecstasy from me.

<hr>

When the weird old butler guy showed up on the morning of the fifth day with an invitation to join our hosts in the west wing of the house, I knew our time of carefree rest was over. It had been an illusion anyway, but a much needed one.

I went in search of the others. Jax and Flynn were easy to find. I eventually heard the sound of trickling water filtering through the half-open door of one of the bathrooms, and followed it to discover Kam and Alex sitting on the floor next to the bathtub. Alex's head was tilted back, her neck resting on the edge of the tub with her long hair trailing into the basin. Kam held a china pitcher from the kitchen filled with water, and was pouring a steady stream over the dark tresses to rinse them.

"This is ridiculous," Alex muttered.

Kam paused. "You want clean hair? Then it isn't ridiculous, you stubborn alpha. You're not getting your hand or your back wet on my watch, so lie back and be pampered, damn it."

I knew I shouldn't be watching like this without announcing my presence, despite the warm, soft feeling the scene engendered. Purposely letting my shoe scuff against the hardwood floor of the hallway, I closed the final two steps to the doorway and knocked lightly on the frame.

"Sorry to interrupt," I said, "but we've been invited into Nikolayev's territory. Hopefully that means Beckett's recovered and it's time to talk."

Alex shot upright like she'd been fired from a cannon, ignoring Kam's huff of irritation as water splashed on the floor. "About bloody time," she said, hauling herself to her feet with her good hand on the tub. Her hair hung in a soaking mass behind her.

"What did I *just* say about getting your back wet?" Kam groused, fumbling for a towel. "We'll be along in a minute, *odama*."

Once everyone was presentable, the butler led us past the grand staircase that divided the two halves of the house, conveying us to the double doors of a beautifully appointed formal receiving room.

"Your guests, sirs," he announced, stepping aside and gesturing at us to enter with his single arm.

We entered to find Kostya Nikolayev standing by the room's massive, unlit fireplace—something which seemed like a bit of an odd feature for a house in the middle of a tropical rainforest. Rhys Beckett sat in an overstuffed chair, wrapped in a flannel dressing gown that practically swallowed his slight frame. He looked drawn, almost frail, but his sea-colored eyes were clear and lucid.

He rose unsteadily at our approach. Nikolayev stepped forward quickly, his hand raised as though to offer support. Beckett waved him away testily.

"Don't hover, Kostya," he said. "It's not as though this was my first heat."

Nikolayev grumbled something inaudible, but backed off—a watchful presence with sharp gray eyes, his long arms folded across his chest.

Beckett immediately turned his attention to us, his expression turning haunted. "Alex. Flynn. I am so incredibly sorry for all of this."

He met us halfway, moving like an old man, and pulled Flynn into a tight embrace. The huge alpha curled around him—a pup with his beloved carrier.

"'S okay, Boss," he said into the smaller man's hair. "No harm done that won't heal. Jax came and rescued us."

"He might have had a *bit* of help with that," Nikolayev put in testily, biting off the words.

"Hush," Beckett said, and I watched in mild amazement from the sidelines as the chairman of the Euro-Soviet Committee hushed.

Beckett released Flynn with a final pat on the back and reached for Alex, taking her good hand in one of his and curling the other around the nape of her neck. "Alex. I'm so sorry. You will have learned about Irina by now, I expect."

Alex leaned down until their foreheads touched and gave a short, wordless nod.

"If I could have thought of a way to tell you without making everything a hundred times more dangerous—" he began.

"It's all right," Alex said hoarsely. "I understand." She eased away. "You're not hurt?"

"No," he said. "No, Alex—I'm fine."

Nikolayev scoffed. "You were kidnapped, drugged, interrogated, tortured psychologically, and thrown into an artificial heat. And I *will* see the one responsible pay in kind."

"We'll get to that part in a minute," Beckett said, letting Alex go. "Jax. Come here."

Jax, too, accepted a hug from the omega who'd been like a parent to him. "Glad you're back, Boss. Not sure I approve in your choice of mates a hundred percent, though. No offense," he added belatedly.

"He's an acquired taste," Beckett replied wryly, "but surprisingly handy to have around in a pinch."

This seemed like as good a time as any to join the conversation.

"When the others said your mate was probably a higher-up in the underground, I'll admit this wasn't quite what I pictured," I told him.

His expression twisted with mild, self-deprecating humor. "Yes. Quite. Though in my defense, it's not as though any of you would have believed the truth."

"About that," I went on, cutting right to the chase. "There are some questions we need answered about dead and tortured alphas and omegas before we go too much further."

"Your sister," Alex said, addressing Nikolayev directly—alpha to alpha. "You faked her death and smuggled her away when she presented as an omega. To protect your own rise to power?"

Nikolayev raised an eyebrow. "My family has been embroiled in the alphomic resistance for generations. Many are betas, holding positions of political and religious power throughout Russia and Eastern Europe. Some, like myself, are alphas hiding in plain sight and embedding ourselves as deeply inside the beta power structure as we can manage. Others are omegas, and have a long history of forging alliances through marriage with other powerful families."

"And the hunts?" I asked. "They weren't real?"

"They were a good way to help fugitives disappear without too many questions being asked." Nikolayev's penetrating gaze pinned me, testing my resolve... seeing if I would give in to my innate omega nature and yield to him. "Dead bodies are not difficult to come by in

Russia. And betas do love a good story of bloodthirsty carnage."

"Are you saying that no alphas or omegas have died at the hands of the Euro-Soviet Committee?" Kam asked, standing straight-backed and firm-shouldered beside me. "Because with all due respect, Chairman, I find that very difficult to believe."

"No," Nikolayev replied. "No, I am not saying that at all. I have stood by and watched innocents fall beneath the firing squad, while sharing drinks and handshakes with the guilty. Believe me when I say, if I had the power to wave a wand and end the bloodshed within the Euro-Soviet Confederacy, I would have done so long before now."

Beckett gave a slow clap. "A lovely speech, dearest. Maybe not the *most* reassuring for our guests—but a good, statesmanlike delivery, nonetheless. And it does rather bring us around to the current point," he finished grimly.

"Which is?" I asked, frowning.

"The Nikolayev family and others like them have spent decades getting to this point without being detected." Beckett's eyes flicked to his mate's for a moment, meeting and holding. "Sloane already suspects. He captured me in hopes of blowing the upper levels of the resistance wide open."

"Did you break under interrogation?" Alex asked, with brutal directness.

A low growl rumbled up from Nikolayev's chest, but Beckett waved him off again.

"Not to my knowledge, which is admittedly spotty at best after they started with the
drugs," Beckett replied, apparently without
offense. "But in the end, it may not matter."

"You were rescued by soldiers in helicopters identifying themselves with secure
Committee codes," Jax said slowly. "Sloane
knows for sure now that there's a rift within
his organization." He turned hard blue eyes on
Nikolayev. "Does he suspect you specifically?"

The Russian's lips twisted. "Of course he
does. He has for years. Despite appearances,
the man is not an idiot."

I thought back over Sloane and Nikolayev's history, looking at it through this new
lens. "He's been shouting from the rooftops
about alphas and omegas infiltrating beta insti-
tutions since he first rose to power." I looked
to Beckett to confirm what I'd just realized.

"And he's absolutely right about that,"
Beckett said tartly. "It's a damn good thing he
comes across as a fringe lunatic most of the
time, or we'd have been in worse trouble than
we already are."

"The underground resistance is not ready
for all-out war," Nikolayev stated with certainty. "However, whether we are ready or not,
that war is coming. It will not be fought with
bombs and bullets. At least, not exclusively. It
will be fought in the hearts and minds of the
people." His eyes landed on me again. "That is

why we need all the allies we can get. Especially ones with your… particular skill set."

"Diplomacy?" I hazarded.

"Persuasion," he replied. "That, and I
need your contacts. Anyone in a position of
power who you believe might harbor alphomic
sympathies."

I thought of all the people I'd met over the
years in the glittering world of international
politics. "I can do that. But that was always the
plan, after Beckett rescued me."

"It's more than that now," Beckett said
kindly. "Be certain you understand what
you're signing up for before you commit."

"Then what are you asking of me?" I
asked, frowning.

The energy in the room shifted as all eyes
focused on our exchange.

Nikolayev ran a speculative gaze over me.
"We are asking you to return to the world
stage openly, as a known omega fugitive. We
are asking you to risk your life in exchange for
all the lives that might be saved if the old order
falls."

My heart skipped a beat. Beside me, I
heard Kam inhale sharply. I didn't dare turn
toward him, choosing instead to lock eyes with
Beckett.

Nikolayev's mate reached out and clasped
my hand in his. "Leona McCready… we're
asking you to be the public figurehead for the
alphomic resistance."

End of Book Two

The *Secret Pack* trilogy concludes in Book
Three: *Truth or Lie.*